A.K. Henderson Books
Black Jack, MO 63033

Email: akhendersonbooks@gmail.com

ISBN-13: 978-0692345351

ISBN-10: 0692345353

CHAPTER 1

"When you don't know who you are, it can do more damage than good."

Try being a teenager growing up in the Harborside Projects of Michigan City, Indiana. The struggle at that place was much like life; it didn't play fair. The environment would either make you or break you to become a hustler, gangster, lame or a nerd. Either way, you had to choose before it chose you.

When it came to Mike Henderson, he didn't choose to be a lame or a hustler. He wanted to be like the other kids. He had the same needs, love, love and more love. With the lack of love, he grew up in a place that treated him unfair. No matter how good he wanted to be, circumstances would not let him. Mike lived with a mother that could not show him what he needed to see, truth was she searched for it herself. She tried, but that was all she did; try. She could not see that their living conditions were taking a toll on her son and family. That wasn't the only thing that caused conflict in the family, her live-in boyfriend, Carlos, also added to the stresses.

To begin with, all Mina and Carlos did was argue. Why couldn't Carlos see that Mina was hurt, sad and depressed? Mike wondered how his mother found energy to put up with him and his abuse. Deciding to think no more of it, he sat on his bed and began to draw, his art was his refuge. While he was in the process of doing his sketches, he heard Carlos yelling. The first thing that came to Mike's mind was, 'He better not lay a hand on my mama.' He waited a few more minutes before continuing to draw. The disagreement became too loud for him to concentrate and Mike again, tried to tune them out. But he couldn't. Just hearing Carlos' tone made him remember what he was told of how Mina met Carlos after Myron's funeral. Since Carlos had come into their lives, he fathered his brother Shawn, and sister Nika, a set of twins.

Closing his eyes, their voices trailed off as Mike thought of how glad he was to be turning seventeen at the end of summer because he could not wait to get out of Indiana. With a sigh, he glanced at the time and saw that it was not time for work yet. Just being in the house alone reminded him of the day his life changed four years ago.

At the age of thirteen, he could not explain his feelings to his mother, and especially not to Carlos. He often examined himself because it was not right for him not to feel love. He assumed that there was something wrong with him. However, it was all made clear that day after school when he found out about his father.

It was a day like every other day, but on that day, something did not feel right when he approached the house. Not sure of what to think of the odd feeling that hung in the air, he decided to go to his mother's room to check on her. Easing open the door, he stood there. In his view was his mother. She sat alone on her huge, red bed with pillows to match, crying her heart out.

As her shoulder length brown hair hung over her shoulders, she sobbed terribly. All kinds of things raced through his mind as he watched his mother cry. Her countenance was that of someone who had lost their best friend. The longer he stood there, the more it killed him to hear his mother in so much pain.

Mina was so in tune with crying that she did not hear him at her door. She did not move a muscle as he continued to watch her. The mood in the room was something he would never forget. Ol' school music blasted throughout the stereo speakers as she lifted her hands to her face. As he went deeper into the room the scent of incense filled the air.

The vision and the smell to Mike was depressing. He didn't know what to think or do. The young man who was barely a teenager found his self-having to comfort the strongest woman he had ever known in the world. He could not understand what was bothering her so and most of all, he had no idea how to comfort her. He finally made his way to the front of his mother. In one hand were tears and in the other, a half emptied bottle of Jack Daniels. She lifted her face towards her son and her eyes were the color of blood. She still tried to smile, but Mike was at a loss of words. He reached up to wipe away her fresh tears and saw trails of old ones upon her cheek. Softly as possible, he asked, "Mama, what's going on here? What's wrong and why are you crying?"

Mina looked up at her son with the saddest pair of eyes and a frown that imprinted on his heart. She patted the spot beside her for him to sit down. Mike's heart raced as he took the seat beside her. The way Mina was acting was unusual for her. Neither he, nor anyone, had ever seen her in such a state.

She had a reputation in the hood everybody in the projects knew that Ms. Mina did not play. She was known for being real and strict. But at that moment she was in rare form. She had a look of despair and hopelessness. The more she stared at him, the more tears paraded down her face. Mike could smell the odor of liquor on her breath when she spoke.

Mina held her son's hands as she said, "Mike, you know I love you with all my heart, but I am about to tell you some things. I hope you understand

and forgive me."

A million things rushed his mind as he waited on her to gather her thoughts. If it hadn't been for the shoe box of pictures he found lying on the bed, Mike would not have thought anything was wrong with this conversation. Unfortunately, that was not the case. Many things were wrong, and finally, he was about to know what it all meant.

Taking a deep breath he mentally prepared himself to listen to her, as he stared into her face. When he looked, he saw guilt, humility and the face of a woman that had done all she could. With a nervous voice and shaky hands, Mina cried a little more as she turned her head from him. He handed her a tissue as her eyes spoke of events that screamed she was guilty.

Without her saying anything he understood his mother on another level more than he ever did before. Trying to save face, Mina smiled and began. "Michael Henderson, you should know that it pains me sometimes to see your face."

When she said that, pain cut Mike's heart like a knife. He had never wanted to be a painful part of his mother's life.

"For a long time, I loved you as much as I hated you."

5

"Huh? Mama, what are you saying?"

"Everything about you reminds me of Chaos, from your facial features, attitude and love for me."

"Mama who is Chaos?" he asked. She wasn't sure if Mike would yank away his hands from hers, therefore, she held onto them tighter. Tears formed in his eyes as he didn't want to let go of her hands either. From the look on her face, he knew what she was saying was truthful but he never knew that his mother felt guilty. Taking away his hands, he patted himself in the chest to say, "Mama, you know I love you."

Mina cried even more as he took her hands back into his. He spoke lovingly in hopes that her body language would change. It did not. All of his life he had been waiting to hear the truth of what Mina had to say, and here it was. It was at that point when he was unsure if he even really wanted to know. Half of him desired to hear it while the other half wished it was all a bad dream.

Mina spoke, "Mike I do love you son, more than anything. I was wrong to harbor those feelings of hate and when I finish, you will understand why. At least, I hope you will."

Trying to sound sure and being a man, Mike said, "Mama I promise you I'm good and I'm listening." Giving his mother his full attention, she

6

smacked her lips and gave his hands a tender squeeze. "Your father was a handsome young Mexican man from Chicago. Everyone called him Chaos." She smiled when she said his name. By the indication of her body language, she was relieving memories of Mike's father. Mina was eight months pregnant when Chaos died. The stress of the whole ordeal sent her into an early delivery. He must have made her smile. She glanced back, and spoke. "The crazy thing about it is that is exactly what he brought to the streets. He was always into something and it didn't take much for him to blow up. When he did, anyone who crossed him paid for it. The thing is, he never intentionally hurt me and he always did what he could for me." Mina turned to Mike to say, "Just like you, Mike. You always do what you can for me but you see, I got tired of the game and wanted him to stop hustling and move with me to Memphis with your Grandma Jean. But your father being who he was, only listened to his friends, mainly Myron."

"Who was Myron? You brought his name up before."

"Oh Mike, Myron was as slick as they came. He had a way with words and could talk himself out of anything."

"That's where you met Carlos right?"

Slowly, and lower than a whisper, she said,

"Yeah." Mina wiped her eyes and then said, "Myron and your father stopped being friends at one point because of me. He was envious of your father because he wanted to be your father. My mistake was, I knew Myron had a thing for me but I was young and flirted with danger. No one knew just how devious Myron was until the day he used Chaos' closest girl against him."

Mina wiped her eyes again and took another shot of liquor. She held her head back and sighed. She looked at Mike and smiled. He knew that she was building up her nerves to say something bad.

"On this particular day, Chaos thought his girl was putting him onto a lick so that he can rob some guy from South Bend, but she wasn't. She went by the info Myron gave her because she didn't think he would lie to her or Chaos when it came to something like that. She really thought he was telling her the truth. Unfortunately, Chaos didn't realize that until it was too late." Mina howled again as she held her head down crying.

Mike spoke, "Mama you have to tell me what happened."

His mother nodded her head. "Chaos didn't discover the scheme until he was caught up in it. He was set up to kill this guy and to be killed so Myron could take over the streets and have me."

It came to Mike as clear as day. His mouth fell open as he said, "Mama, you set my father up?"

Mina did not answer. She only cried harder and harder. Mike wanted to snatch his hands away from her for being a fool. How could she not see? How could she have been so blind to what Myron was using her for? All kinds of emotions overcame him. From that moment on, Mike vowed not to trust another woman. In his eyes they were weak and deemed untrustworthy.

Mina then said, "It wasn't until after it all happened that I, like everyone else, found out that Myron set the whole thing up. He not only played everybody against the other, but he ran his mouth one time too many. Some gangsters from Chicago found out that Myron was behind it and they had him stretched out for what he did to your father."

"But mama, why did you go to the funeral?" Mike questioned. If she had not gone to the funeral, she would not have met Carlos but then again they wouldn't have had Shawn and Nika. It was a win lose situation for him.

Mina said between cries and sniffles, "I don't want to talk about it anymore. It hurts too bad."

"Mama don't do this to me right now. Why would you go to that man's funeral knowing what he did?" he pleaded.

Mina looked at him and finally told him, "I had to make sure he was actually dead. I hated myself for what I did but I wasn't going to rest until I saw them put him in the ground. That's why." He was unsure of his own actions as he took everything she said in. Tighter than before, he held onto his mother's hand and gave it a sensible squeeze.

Mike did not leave her side. After she wiped her eyes and blew her nose again, Mina gazed at her son as if she wanted him to say something. But Mike got up without saying a word to his distraught mother. In actuality, words could not form as he began to digest the story she had told him.

Going back to his room meant safety to him. He learned that being alone was the best place to be. He closed the door and sat on his bed. Since that day, Mike looked at his mother different. He couldn't understand how she allowed herself to be caught in the middle but he knew she was only doing what she thought was right. Mike wanted to find out more about the real story of Chaos, but he knew that when gangsters were involved, he was not going to get anywhere.

The sound of cars passing by interrupted his trip down memory lane. It still amazed Mike how often he would think about that turning point in his life. He could close his eyes and still see it as fresh as if it were yesterday. Feeling like he was going to cry all over again, he blinked his eyes and realized Mina and Carlos arguing caused him to reminisce as well as be late for work. He got up, cleaned his face and left out his room.

He closed the front door behind him, and ran to catch the city bus. When he paid his token, he took the nearby seat and stared out the window as the bus pulled off. He was glad to be out of the eleventh grade and close to graduating, he was also thankful for the job his friend's uncle arranged for him. The more blocks the bus drove, the more he stared out the window contemplating his life.

Lately, all he did was daydream about things getting better and being able to leave home. He never liked Carlos and believed the feeling was mutual. And from the way things were going at home, he knew that it would be a matter of time before Carlos pushed him over the edge.

The bus came to Mike's stop. He got off the bus and clocked in. Working at a burger joint wasn't the best but it was a job. He still had his life on his mind and hoped the customers would help ease his mind as he worked. Wishful thinking did not help at all that day, it seemed like the customers were worse than ever. Everybody complained for one reason or another, and if it wasn't for the fact that he was saving his money to leave Indiana, he would have already quit.

Like most teenagers you would think he would be talkative with people his age, but he was not. He didn't care too much for his co-workers. Although everyone from his high school worked there, Mike laid low. Many of them were too conceited and wasteful in their own right. Although he stayed because he needed the money, there was another reason his job was worthwhile. The reason's name was Lida. To Mike, she was the most beautiful creature he had ever seen. Everything about her was perfect and to see other guys trying to get at her, almost made him mad.

But why not? She was gorgeous, he observed her shiny, but flawless dark skin, medium grey eyes and thick wavy hair. Her accent had a southern charm to it, Louisiana to be exact. Just to hear her speak did something to him.

Behind all that beauty, he wondered what kind of person she really was. The girl of his dreams could be kind of stuck up at times. She spoke her mind and it was what it was. But Mike had a thing for stuck up females. It was something about chicks with attitude that he loved, and Lida was no exception. In reality, he was a shy guy and didn't think he could even approach a female, especially Lida.

In his eyes Lida was the epitome of sexy and she was two years older than him. Everything about her told him she was out of his league. It didn't stop the many smiles she gave him when she caught him staring at her. To Mike, it was a cat and mouse game.

Distracting his glances at Lida was his brother, Shawn. Mike knew basketball practice was over as soon as he walked in. With a brief smile and smirk, Shawn walked over to where Mike was and asked, "What up bro?"

Mike did not say anything. He was lost in one of his many daydreams of Lida. Shawn looked at Mike, and then followed his eyes to see what he was looking at. Mike felt Shawn's eyes and trying to play it off, he replied, "Hey what's up Shawn?"

"Nothing but watching you do the same thing you're doing every time I come in here."

"I'm working every time you come in here."

"More like stalking."

"Man, I am not stalking nobody. I'm doing my job. I have to make sure the customers are enjoying their food."

"Yeah?"

"Yeah."

"Then why every time you so-called check out everything, it happens to be where that same girl is?"

Mike had to think of something fast. He replied, "Because she always works in the area I'm checking out." Shawn laughed. Mike didn't think he bought it but he really didn't care. He did not want to have that conversation right now, Mike quickly asked Shawn, "Where Nika at?" He knew she was standing outside with his co-worker Tiny, but he had to get Shawn's mind off talking about him.

"You don't see her?" Shawn said as he pointed to his sister and her girlfriend outside the door.

"Oh my bad, I didn't see her at first."

"Mike, how you not see her? She is outside talking to Tiny right over there where you were just looking. You goofy."

"Man for real, I didn't see her at first."

"Bet you didn't."

As he and his brother watched their sister, Mike looked back and forth at them both. He envied their connection, they shared the same parents and the same birthday. His brother and sister were inseparable. They even get sick together, Mike thought with a smile. Looking at his watch, he knew they were early, so he asked, "Y'all bout to order or you coming in here to kill time?"

"Naw, mama said for us to catch the city bus with you and not walk to grandma's."

"Why not?"

"I don't know man. There's no telling when it comes to mama."

"When I left the house, she didn't say anything to me about it."

"You know how mama can be."

"True, but what you mean is, you know how Carlos can be!" Mike said frankly as he continued to watch his sister and Tiny talking. He desired so much to know what they were discussing. More importantly, he needed to find out how close Lida was to Tiny and how that could help him with her.

Shawn asked as he kept his gaze, "What time you get off because I'm ready to go home and take a shower?"

"In about ten minutes, but the bus doesn't come for another half hour, unless you want us to walk."

The late bus was often times his cop out so he would miss out on all of the arguing at home. He hated to hear it, and that was why, as much as possible, he stayed away.

Interrupting his thoughts, Shawn stated, "I'm too tired for all that right now. So walking is out of the question."

They laughed at that. Mike suggested, "Well, your feet won't feel any better standing here waiting on me."

"You right, I'm going to wait outside, come get me when you're ready."

"Ok, I will be out in a few minutes."

Shawn left, and Mike watched the clock and counted down the minutes before he was to meet his brother and sister. He was getting off and wished he could just walk to Southgate to his grandmothers. He gave one last look to Lida and she smiled back.

CHAPTER 2

Lida was born and raised in Baton Rouge, Louisiana, Bayou Country. For the longest time, it had always been her mom, Diane, her grandmother, Rosy, her brother, Corey and herself. As far as her dad Ricky was concerned, Lida didn't remember much of him. However, she did recall how good he smelled, how he stayed chewing on a tooth pick and all of the advice he gave her.

While on break in her own little place, she heard a co-worker say to another, "You have to always be there for your man."

The statement brought back memories of the last conversation she had with her dad. Ricky went to prison two weeks after her seventh birthday. It was the night she was coming home from bible study with her grandmother. The whole neighborhood was out covering the entire street. They didn't know what was happening so they stood back and watched like everyone else.

The noise from the crowd drowned out Lida's soft voice as she asked Rosy what was going on. The night was busy as the police and FBI made their way through the neighborhood trying to make everybody stay back. Lida, young and nosy, tried her best to see through the crowd. As soon as she made it closer to the front, she saw her mother standing on the front porch crying frantically, begging the uniformed officers not to take her husband away.

Lida had never seen her mother so terrified and the onlookers did not make Ricky's departure any better. She wiggled trying to get loose from Rosy's grip so Rosy held her hand tighter. When Lida saw her father come into view, he was bound in shackles from head to feet. Her mother reached for him as the police held her back. It was at that moment she knew something was incredibly wrong.

With all her might, she broke free from Rosy's grip. In her ear, she heard her screaming, "Lida, come back here!"

Too late, she made her way towards her house. Diane saw her and ran towards her daughter. The police ran over to stop her but she told them who Lida was. They stood down and allowed the duo to reconnect. Seconds later, grandma Rosy walked over and they watched as her father was put in the back of a police car, and carried away. Diane took Lida inside. Lida had never seen their home in such a mess. It looked like the police came in and flipped everything over. Furniture was tossed all around and the door was even kicked off the hinges. The house was a complete catastrophe. Miraculously, her brother Corey slept through the entire ordeal.

While Ricky was awaiting his transfer to the federal facility, the family wasn't allowed to see him. They were allowed only one phone call. The day he called, he talked to them each for a minute. When it became Lida's turn, she cried as she grabbed the phone. "Daddy I miss you so much, please come home!"

"Cupcake, I'm sorry but I can't, but just because I am not there does not mean I don't love you."

"I love you too, daddy."

"Would you do me a favor?"

"Sure daddy."

"Take care of your mother and your brother and remember that family comes first."

"I will but daddy, mommy won't talk to me. I just want her to stop crying, I don't know what to do."

"Don't worry yourself honey, mommy just needs some time. She has a lot on her mind. It's going to be hard for her to take care of you and your brother without me."

"Ok."

"And make sure you do good in school and

remember, don't ever depend on a man to take care of you. If a man is willing to take care of you, let him, but be your own person. If that man asks you to be there for him, do that. Don't let anybody tell you what you can't do, you do what you have to and take care of yourself. Just don't let any man mess you over, you hear me?"

"I hear you daddy."

"Don't give your mom any trouble. Now hurry up and give her back the phone."

"I love you daddy."

"I love you too, cupcake."

In the days that followed, as Diane became so caught up in what Ricky was going through, her children became neglected. Lida tried not to give her mother any trouble, but she was hurting too. She needed to feel like her mother still cared, just like anyone else, but she wasn't getting that attention.

After about a month after the phone call, her mother never talked about hearing from her father again. In fact, as the first few years passed, many men came and went. Most tried to play daddy just to get with Diane, but Lida wasn't buying it. She became more outspoken and rebellious, lying and sneaking around. Lida didn't care anymore because all she wanted was her father back home.

She became a handful for her mother. One morning Diane thought Lida was asleep and she overheard her talking to Rosy. "I don't want the children to be far from their daddy."

"Child what is the difference? He told you to go on with your life. None of you can see him anyway. It's not like he's going to get out and come after you all."

"I know mama, but Lida is taking it hard."

"Well, sit her down and explain to her what is about to happen."

"I tried, but ever since Ricky talked to her on the phone she hasn't been the same."

"Diane, some of it could be because she sees men coming and going. Having men trying to play daddy to an impressionable girl, it don't help it only makes things worse."

"But I have to support them."

"You also have to be strong."

"It's hard ma."

"I know. So what exactly did they lock Ricky up for?"

"Drug trafficking through the ports, which was part of some so-called drug ring. He was only trying to give back to the neighborhood. Everyone in the streets knows that my husband was all about being there and taking care of business."

"What he did was wrong."

"Mama people lie, steal and do underhanded stuff all day, every day. My husband only wanted what is best for his family and the community. If he said he was there for you, he was there for you."

"I hear you Diane but the end doesn't always justify the means!"

"Yeah mama, but fifty years in the federal prison and no parole. We can't even see him."

"How is that?"

"The last time he and I talked, he told me not to come see him. He said he doesn't want his children to see him caged like some animal."

"Does Lida know? I know Corey is too young to understand."

"No but what else can I do?"

"Come to Michigan City with me. You can start over while they are still young."

"I don't know mama."

"What else is there not to know?"

"Louisiana is all I know, I love it here."

"So do I, but when something better comes along, you have to take it."

"I talked to Dooney's mother and she said Corey can stay with her until you can get yourself together. This would be a great opportunity for you and Lida to reconnect before she gets more out of control."

Having heard enough, Lida went back to her room and cried. She didn't understand, in her eyes her loving father only did good things and he was being punished for it. She truly believed nothing was left for them in Louisiana without him. As much as she didn't like the idea of leaving she wiped her tears and vowed to one day figure out why people she loved did what they did. But for now nothing mattered anymore.

She was going to be stronger than her mother was and keep the promises she made to her dad. With nothing more left tying them to Louisiana, the three of them packed up and left. Corey would come and join them later. 'No use in crying now, I guess I have to deal with it.' Lida thought, as her grandma Rosy got off of the exit from I-94E. The sign read Michigan City. She didn't think they were going to Indiana because of the sign. It was the strangest place they had ever seen.

23

Lida would never forget that day. It was a hot summer's day and it appeared that everyone in the city was on Michigan Boulevard to welcome them. Lida wasn't sure if she would like it, but the people did make them feel at home. As time passed and she adjusted to the neighborhood, she began to memorize the street names so in case she got lost she would be able to tell someone where she lived.

Right away the first thing she remembered was the big water tower she didn't live too far from it. The boys on the block weren't too bad, but the girls; they didn't like her. For reasons of their own, they taunted her for her southern accent, darker skin and her hair. They just could not believe that a dark skinned girl could have real long hair like hers and it not be weave.

It seemed every week, Lida was engaged in a fight and soon the streets made her out to be someone she never thought she'd become. The next few years weren't any easier because she was still considered the new kid. But all that changed when she met Tiny. They became thick as thieves and she even helped Lida when the light skinned girls tried to jump her or threaten to cut her hair.

Before Tiny, she never thought she would be happy about her new life. She and Michigan City had a love hate relationship. The thought of not seeing Baton Rouge haunted her, but Lida still maintained and was determined to keep her promise to Ricky. Lida pressed through and with Tiny by her side and she and her mother reconnecting, things worked out. She didn't think she could do it, but she did. She finally graduated high school and turned nineteen a month after school. However, today of all days, she felt sad and didn't want to be at work. Sometimes it was hard for her to get out of bed, thinking about her dad put a damper on her day. She was thankful that her girl Tiny helped her get the job, but it was also a sad time because Tiny would be leaving for school soon. With all the hours she was working, she rarely hung out with her best friend. Contemplating Tiny leaving, she spoke softly to herself, "I need me a boo thang or something this lonely stuff ain't where it's at."

To her, Tiny was like family and she was tired of family leaving her. If she didn't need the money, she would hang out with her girl, but business comes first. She had to help Rosy take care of Corey who was now fifteen, ever since Diane died from cancer the year before. Then she thought about what it was about her job that she hated, as customers continued to come in.

Guys often pretended to order food just to ask for her number. She couldn't stand fake people. To her, the guys were all the same. She thought, you would think that time and age would change people, but it didn't.

Lida assumed these goofies didn't seem to get the fact that she was not a water head like most. She was far more mature than the girls her age, and she wasn't into the hoods like Tiny was. Shaking her head in disgust, she got up and went to the back to get something from her purse. The first face she saw was Mike's.

He was sort of a lame, but very cute. He was quiet and kept to himself. He kind of reminded her of her father with his hazel eyes and long cornrows. She noticed that Mike always had his brother and sister around, which to her screamed family man. Tiny even told her that she's caught him staring at her when she was not paying attention. She had already decided she would give him a chance if he came at her right, but he never did.

It did not bother her at all that she was two years his senior, there was something different about him, something in the way he smiled at her. Her day could be going horrible and seeing his smile would make it go by with ease. He seemed to care about those he kept around him and with the right woman in his life, she knew he would be the complete package. To Lida, Mike had an innocence about him that was so inviting. His demeanor didn't make her think he was a player or the sneaky type. If the opportunity presented itself, maybe one day he would talk to her and she would give him a chance. But up until now it's never happened.

She wanted to see for herself where his head was. She got up to go over to him to try and break the ice, but at that precise time, Mike walked off. Lida unfazed, turned back to her seat to finish her break. She didn't know that he had seen her coming his way. Seeing that his time was up at work, he avoided an awkward situation and in a quick dash, he hurried to clock out. He was not ready to have her approach him yet. Keeping his head down and eyes off Lida, he went outside and met up with Shawn. He couldn't believe that she had thought to come over and say something to him.

Doing his best to brush off the funny feeling in his stomach from almost talking to the girl of his dreams, laughingly he asked Shawn, "You ready to go?"

"I am," Shawn answered.

"Where's Nika at? She knows it's time to leave."

"She over there," Shawn pointed out.

Nika was still talking to Tiny, she was about fifty feet from them. Mike yelled out, "Nika come on here. I don't have time to be waiting on you. You had the last ten minutes to run your mouth. Hurry up and let's go."

"I'm coming. Dang you hella goofy!" She

yelled as she turned back to say goodbye to Tiny. Nika jogged to catch up to her brothers. Mike reached and put his arm around her and gave her a hug, she cringed and said, "Why you over here rushing me, ugh!? You smell like that nasty food you be making all day."

Popping his collar, Mike said as the twins laughed, "Naw miss me with that, Nika. I smell like money, something you don't have."

She realized he was right. She smiled and said, "I'm just playing."

"Yea I bet you were."

She told him that because she knew her brother may take it personal, he was just that type. In her playful tone, she asked, "Y'all want to go to the firework show next week?"

"You know we don't have money to get in and I am not sneaking in. It is not worth all the trouble we went through last year just to see it," Shawn spoke as he cut his eyes toward Mike.

"Well, I want to see it."

"I do too Nika, but it cost to get in and we don't have it."

"I get tired of not having no money. All my friends are going to be there." Nika pouted.

"I feel you on that, but there is nothing we can do about it."

"I wish there was though."

Mike gave them a critical look, he was anti-social and going to the beach being around all those people was the last thing he wanted to do. He knew that every year, everyone who was anyone came out to show off their cars and new 4th of July outfits. It was almost like a hood parade. Everyone he didn't talk to would be there and they would be the main ones frontin'. Besides, he knew Lida would be there and he didn't want to see anyone pushing up on her.

The twins always tried to get Mike to spend money on them. They couldn't run game on him, but sometimes he allowed them to think they did, mainly because he got tired of them trying so hard. As much as he disliked their dad Carlos, he would not take it out on them. Mike knew his siblings were not like their dad, and he would do anything he could to make them happy.

He was the big brother and part of his responsibility was to watch out for them. It did get old though. Giving into their plot, he stated nonchalantly, "I tell you what. I get paid that Friday, I can pay y'all's way in if you both be quiet about it."

Nika acted so surprised, she screamed with happiness. "Seriously big bro? You got us? I mean, you dropping some cash for us at a firework show? You the best!"

Pretending as she did, Mike stated, "Why wouldn't I? Quit acting like you didn't know I was going to offer anyway. At least this way, you won't have to watch your back the whole time."

"That's why you my favorite brother."

"Shawn, I'm your only brother."

"Yeah you are, you know that!"

They all laughed. When they made it to the bus stop, Nika gave her big brother a hug. This time it was sincere, she knew Mike was saving all he had to leave the city and for him to spend it on them meant he was still going to take care of them. She already knew it. Mike had never let them down and he always did what he could.

The twins knew he had every reason to be ugly to them because of their father. But he wasn't. Mike didn't have his dad like they did and they could not imagine growing up with their parents not together, even if their dad was mean some times. The sound of the bus brakes interrupted her thoughts. Mike being a gentleman, let her on the bus first.

He and Shawn walked on afterwards. While on the bus, Shawn looked over at Mike and said,

"Mike, Michigan City isn't that bad when you think about it."

"Shawn this is the only place you have lived. Of course, it's not that bad. What do you have to compare it to?"

"Yeah Shawn, if you lived in Gary or Hammond, you would freak out."

"No I wouldn't. I'm a G, I ain't scared of nobody and plus the ladies love me."

"Shawn, it's not about all that. First of all, you are not hard and secondly these females are trying to be in love and stuff. To them it's about loving the one you have and getting that love back."

"Why you always talking about love Mike? You don't know nothing about that. I am beginning to think you are one of those Keith Sweat type of dudes."

Nika butted in to say, "Shawn while you playing, that is what the women like. Go head Mikey!"

Shawn responded, "And what exactly is that Nika? What do y'all want?"

"Women want a man that loves her more than his homeboys and not just that, he treats her like a queen. He's not all about sex and he's not afraid to say he loves her. He keeps his promises and he makes her feel important."

Shaking his head, Shawn teased, "Hopeless romantic. Y'all better go somewhere with that. Nika you watch too much TV. Where you going to find him at, in a magazine?"

Nika spoke with assurance as Shawn laughed, "Boy boo! God is going to send him, that's all you need to know."

Mike didn't say a word as he listened to them go back and forth. He had never thought of being a man like that, but it did sound good. He glanced at his sister with a smile. The bus dropped them off at the corner, two houses down from theirs. The trio didn't make it close to the driveway before they heard glass breaking.

The sound was all too familiar to them. They all looked at each other, as if to say, 'Not again.' As usual Carlos and Mina were at it again. From the sounds they heard as they crept closer to the house, they knew it was serious. They walked slowly toward the window, trying not to attract attention to them. Peeping inside they could see Carlos towering over their mother.

He yelled out, "What the hell were you doing down there with them fools on Cedar? Huh? You ain't got no business being over there."

"Baby, it wasn't like that." She pleaded.

"I don't care what it was like. No woman of mine is going to be hanging around a bunch of bums." Mina cried as he said, "Shut up. And if I catch you there again, on my mama I will kill you. You hear me!?"

Mina didn't say a word. They all knew she was terrified of Carlos and if she answered, he would only get angrier. He stared into her face and hatefully stated, "Keep on testing me and watch what I do. I already want to kill you, just give me a reason."

A sound was heard by the window. Mina turned her eyes in that direction to see her children. She gave them a reassuring look hoping the children wouldn't be afraid. That did not help. She was worried because she did not want Mike to pop off and do something stupid. And at this point, Carlos had given him plenty of reason to do just that.

Instead, it was Shawn that ran through the door screaming, "Mama! Mama!"

Mike and Nika ran in behind him. Carlos pushed Shawn to the side and found himself locked in a stare down with Mike. He did not care about Carlos' mood. He wasn't going to keep standing by and watching this go on. Mina and Mike both knew it. Mina could see Mike's face turning red and his fist balled up. He wasn't backing down this time and neither was Carlos. It was about to go from bad to worse at any second and before it could, Mina got up and stepped in between them saying, "Y'all go to your rooms. I will be there in a minute."

Mina took Shawn's arms from around her, and Nika and Mike both gave her disappointed looks. Mina saw it in their faces, but could not allow this to go any further. Mike let Shawn and Nika go first past Carlos. Every kind of emotion swelled inside as he walked past Carlos.

His brother and sister's worthless father continued to stare and breathe hard as he listened to Mina do her best to convince Mike to walk away. The very moment he made it to Carlos he stopped and looked back giving one last menacing look. Mike's heart was full of rage as he continued to his room slowly, ready for Carlos to say or do something else. Mina saw the glare in his eyes and spoke, "Go on to your room Mike. I will be there in a minute."

Mike turned his head and went on behind his siblings. When they got out of Mina and Carlos' ear shot, Nika spoke quietly, "I hope mama is alright."

"Me too. I wish we could go to grandma Jean house." Mike ignored what they were saying and continued toward his room. He was in a zone now as he walked into his room and flopped down on his bed. He could hardly keep himself from screaming as his thoughts rambled through his head. He knew that if things did not change, he would kill Carlos or vice-versa.

After a few moments of hateful thinking, he reconsidered, telling himself that he couldn't do that to Shawn and Nika. Carlos was their father, even if he didn't like the man. There was a light knock at the door. Grabbing his cover, he wiped his face and cleared his throat and answered, "Who is it?"

Poking her head through the doorway was his mother. Her face was somewhat content, but he knew she could fake that feeling just to protect her children.

"Can I come in?" Mike nodded his head. Taking her time, she sat next to him and placed her arm around him. Mike laid his head on her shoulder and instantly felt comforted. "Baby you ok?"

Mike did not answer. He would not allow her the satisfaction of getting him to pour his heart out. Mina went on to speak more. "I am sorry you had to see that. You know sometimes adults argue and say things they don't mean." Mike still remained silent. He only listened. Mina kissed the top of his head, and said, "Mike. I love you and I promise you, it is going to get better."

Mike lifted his head and got on one knee in front of his mother. "When mama? How are you going to make me believe that time is coming? Am I going to have to kill this fool in order for you and us to be safe?"

"Baby don't say that."

"Why not? You always take up for him and I can't stand it. You always come to us trying to make us believe that Carlos didn't mean what he said or did this time. You know like we know, he means everything he says.

I swear to you mama I'm over it and there's nothing you can say to fix this. He does not love you or us. Look at the way he treats you. How do you look at this man and see love? Do not sit and tell me it's going to get better!" Mike had to catch himself, he noticed his voice getting louder. "You have been telling us that for as long as I can remember and we're still in the same situation."

Mina did not answer his charges. She could not answer them. She simply said, "Just be patient and believe it is going to get better."

"How much longer do you think we are going to sit here and watch him do you like this? How much do you honestly believe we can take?" Mina knew her son was right, but she was not going to admit that he was. From the angry glare he gave her, she knew he was serious. Mike proclaimed, "When I get married, I'm going to make sure my wife will never go through this."

Mina hugged and kissed him on the forehead. She then said, "Mike, please don't look at me like that."

What she saw at the moment was Chaos, the resemblance had never been so strong. Mina knew she was not going to be able to talk any sense into her oldest son. Carefully, Mina got off the bed.

When she made it to the door, Mike said, "Grandma told me to treat people how we want them to treat us. I guess some people never learn."

Mina hung her head and left out his bedroom door and continued to the twins' rooms. Mike laid back in his bed and covered his head to muffle his cries and fell asleep.

The next morning he was prepared for the nice Carlos to show up and like he assumed, it happened. He would always try to be cool with everybody after a blowout like last nights. "What up lil' man?"

Mike thought about screaming, 'I hate you!' but that would only ruin his own day. Never had he thought that it was ever possible to hate someone like he did at that moment. Grunting through his teeth, he replied, "Man kick rocks."

Carlos saw the look on his face and thought twice about saying anything else and Mike was glad he saw it. Carlos didn't say another word to Mike as he walked out the door and headed to work.

Mike's day brightened up when he saw the beautiful Lida in the dining area. Whenever Lida was around, he was no longer concerned about whatever may have been bothering him that day. With each passing moment he considered approaching her but never worked up the nerve. He was ready but then again, he wasn't sure if he even wanted the conversation to happen.

Mike had just gotten to the point of not even caring anymore. What was the worst she could do, say no? Nothing was going right for him and if she treated him like she treated the others, it wouldn't hurt too bad. His life was already not at the best, and nothing she could do would bring it down any lower.

CHAPTER 3

When he glanced up, Lida was staring at him like he usually did her. It was odd to have her make him the center of attention. She must have noticed him looking back at her because she got up and walked over. The pep talk to himself came quickly. 'Straighten up boy. Don't stare! Calm down. Get it together. Smile.' When he looked up again she was right in front of him. Her eyes were grayer than he ever seen. Her perfume overwhelmed his senses as he took in her scent. How perfect was she!?

The next thing he heard was the sweet sound of her voice saying, "Hey Mikey, how you doing?"

Giving her his best smile he could muster up, he replied casually, "I'm good. How you doing?"

"I'm good just tired."

Just saying those few words unnerved him. Goose bumps sprouted all over him and if she wasn't standing so close to him, he might have thrown up. He took a deep breath and then responded, "Tired of what?"

"Never mind. I'm good, but I've been having the feeling that you want to say something to me. Is this true?"

39

"You had the feeling that I want to say something to you, huh?"

"Um hmm. So express yourself. Tell me what is on your mind, or you can't talk like you are doing now?"

He gave her a smile slightly embarrassed. She really didn't need to know how much he adored her. Trying to play it cool he said, "Uh, I saw you looking at me and uh…"

"And uh what?"

The drive thru bell rang just in time, he swiftly took the chance for a getaway as he glanced over at the window. He finished, "And uh, I got to go tend to the customers."

Giving him one last chance to speak, she was hesitant then said, "Alright, guess I will talk to you later ok?"

Mike faintly said ok as he rushed away from her. He needed to get his self together as he went to help a customer. He had a feeling she was still standing there staring. As the day wore on, Mike could not get the meeting between them out his head. Throughout the day he thought about picking up where he left off. Moments later while he was on break, Tiny made her way over to him. Jokingly she inquired, "So I hear you like my girl Lida?"

That caught him completely off guard. Mike got nervous all over again. His eyes grew big. He tried to disguise it by moving to a nearby seat as he questioned, "Who? Who told you that?"

"That nervous grin on your face did."

"You watch too many crime shows. Me looking nervous don't mean nothing, look how you came at me."

"No you are too obvious." Mike was quiet and Tiny continued, "Be honest. You like her or what? Either you do or you don't!"

He smiled at Tiny and thought that Lida approaching him was the reason for her line of questions. Maybe she wanted to know the answer to the same questions. "I guess she a'ight."

"You guess she a'ight? What kind of answer is that?"

He knew she wasn't feeling his attempt to play it cool. Mike recanted, "Yeah I'm feeling her, but I'm not into chasing after nobody. Why did she say something to you?"

Tiny smirked thinking, 'I know something you don't,' Tiny toying with him said, "From the way she was talking to me, I don't think it will be much of a chase."

"Girl don't be playing with me about her. If I did think she liked me, I would try to holla at her, but we will see."

"Boy stop it, everybody sees you staring at her but anyways I will talk to you later." "A'ight."

Once he got off his break, he replayed both conversations he had with Lida and Tiny in his head. His imagination got the best of him, then came thoughts about his first date with her, their first kiss and by the end of shift, he had envisioned his marriage proposal to her.

After five o'clock, he clocked out hoping that things at home wouldn't be hectic. After catching the bus, he made it home and noticed the house was a mess. "Man what is all this? These fools stay fighting."

Mike walked through the house calling out for everyone, and no one answered. It was then when he stumbled across his mother lying on the floor lifeless it seemed. At first his feet would not move as he tried to go to her, eventually they took life and allowed him to run to his mother's aid.

"Mama! Get up please. Oh God, mama please be alright. Please don't take my mama. Mama, please, please, wake up!"

The only thing he could think of was that

Carlos had a part in it. Then Mina moaned a little, and he ran over to the phone and dialed 911. He cried uncontrollably as the operator kept asking questions.

Everything was a blur from that point on as the paramedics rushed inside their home. When they arrived Mina was still breathing, but was unresponsive. Mike had already managed to call his grandmother, who rushed over when she heard about her daughter. Seeing that the medics had Mina stable she did not go to the hospital right away. She stayed with Mike while he tried to find Shawn and Nika. Mike wondered where they could be. Suddenly he heard soft, whimpering sounds coming from the closet in the kitchen.

Quietly he summoned his grandmother to come closer. Taking his time, he eased the door open. Trembling, crying and hugging each other were his brother and sister. Mike extended his hand as they came out of the closet. Jean greeted the two and held them tightly as she tried to calm them down.

Mike then asked, "What happened?"

Nika spoke hoarsely to say, "Mama and daddy started arguing. Daddy got mad when mama said something about us leaving. Daddy just started going crazy."

"Mikey we tried to stop him, but we couldn't. He was too strong," Shawn said.

Nika explained further, "He smacked Shawn and mama was hitting him and when she jumped on his back, he threw her down. Then we ran and hid in the closet. After that we heard mama screaming then it got quiet."

Hearing that broke Mike's heart. He knew that Carlos could do some crazy things, but that was an all-time low for hitting his own children. He glared at his brother and sister and asked, "You both ok though?" They both nodded and said yes. This incident fueled the rage that brewed inside Mike. Killing Carlos was the only thing on his mind, but he had to be smart about it.

Jean placed her arms around her grandchildren and said, "You two go pack some clothes, you are coming with me." Shawn and Nika did as she asked. Turning toward Mike, Jean said, "You are the man of the house now. I'll take you to the hospital, I know God's going to take care of my baby. I need you to go check on her and let her know you all are ok. I will get them situated."

Everyone left the house with Jean, heading towards St. Anthony's Hospital. She dropped Mike off and headed home. He walked in and stopped at the receptionist desk and was directed to the waiting area. A little while later Jean and the twins arrived, the doctor walked out and spoke to them. When the doctor told them she was in a coma, they all cried and were devastated.

Mike's body shook all over, but he stayed strong as the doctor told them that it was not because of anything physical, it was the stress that caused her to have a stroke. Carlos was dead in Mike's mind. They were told that stress of life's situation caused her to have an aneurism and her situation was a touch and go.

The days came and went as the police searched for Carlos who disappeared in the midst of all the confusion at the house. He had warrants, so there was no telling where he was and if he would return. During this time Mike became dead on the inside and he spent more late nights in the streets trying to keep his mind off of what had happened. He was becoming something he never wanted to be, just like Carlos. He stalked the streets angry and short tempered. Carlos being on the loose had him spooked and paranoid. One night while Mike was on the west side hustling, he found himself cornered by a group of young wannabe thugs. He had lost track of time and knew he shouldn't have been on that part of town by himself. The group had every intention to rob him but Mike wasn't going down without a fight. It was four against one and Mike picked the loudest one in the group and stole on him breaking his nose. The others rushed him and unleashed a fury of punches and kicks. Mike looked around trying to find an escape route. As soon as he had the chance he was going to make a run for it.

Suddenly he heard footsteps approaching from behind the group. The sound of a 9 mm chambering a round made them all freeze. "Fellas this here don't look like a fair one. Maybe we should even things out so the little homie can have a chance. What y'all think?"

The man talking stood in a black hoodie and black military cargo pants and black Nike boots. The brim of a black New York Yankees fitted cap covered his eyes.

"Yo that's Cali." the youth with the broken nose whispered to another. "You got it big homie, we ain't on nothing. We was just leaving." The leader of the group said.

Cali nodded and lowered his pistol to his side as the group turned and took off down a nearby alley. Cali helped a battered Mike up off of the ground. "What's your name homie?" Mike stared at the stocky goon briefly before responding. "Mike…my name is Mike. Yo man thanks for you know, helping me with that."

"No problem my dude. What you doing over here hustling naked? I ain't never seen you around here before, where you from?" Mike still trying to get his wits about him, looked around to make sure there were no other surprises.

"I'm from Harborside but my mom lives in Eastport." Cali acknowledged by nodding again. "Alright, well if you gonna be out here you can't be by yourself. If anything, you need to be strapped homie. I'ma get you right, let me give you a ride back to the east side."

"A'ight, man thanks again. I owe you big time."

The two got more acquainted as they headed to the other side of town. Mike didn't know it but Cali had saved his life in more than one way. His heart was hardened and he didn't know if he could trust Cali but the way he came through for him showed he was legit.

The more Mike visited his mother, the more he became bitter inside. Just the thought of losing his mother at seventeen got to him. Even with all the things Carlos had put her and them through, seeing her in a hospital was not something he looked forward to.

His grandmother was worried that he might do something to get himself in trouble. He was still pissed about everything, but he knew Shawn and Nika needed him to be strong and that was what he planned to do regardless of how he felt about the situation. Thinking about his mother, he knew he loved her and he wanted her to be happy, and he wanted her to know that she had her family behind her.

After being by Mina's side for over two weeks, she finally woke up. It was the day they hoped she would see just how bad her life was and make a change. In fact, she told them that things would be different for the better and she loved them all.

Grandma Jean leaned in closer to her daughter and rubbed her head with anointing oil on her. Jean spoke saying, "Child you don't know how blessed you are, do you? Mina God loves you, and I'm going to tell you something you need to stop testing him or you're going to end up getting exactly what you're asking for."

"I know mama and I intend on getting myself together. Thank you so much for taking care of the kids. I love you for that."

They all bowed their heads as Jean prayed for Mina. The words she spoke in prayer touched them all except for Mike. He felt those words weren't for him, if God really cared about him or his family he wouldn't allow these things to be happening. He wanted to cry, but his pride would no longer let him. Once she finished praying for Mina, he knew things would never be the same.

While Mina was in the hospital, they found

out that Carlos was in police custody for a robbery he committed years before, as well as the assault on Mina. He was awaiting trial, and that was a good thing. Mina remained in the hospital going through rehab and the twins were at Jean's. They all pulled together and tried to return their lives back to normal. Grandma Jean kept telling them prayer changes things, but Mike wasn't trying to hear it. If there was any prayer he wanted to have answered, it was that Mina kept her word.

Continuing to go to work for Mike was not easy. But he was in need of something to keep himself occupied. That Friday when he went to get his check, Lida was working the register. He knew his attitude had been horrible lately and he had been short with her, but Lida never tripped about it. Mike noticed that her being around kept him calm. Seeing her made his day. He approached her and said nervously, "Hey Lida, what's up with you?"

"Hey baby, what's up?"

Clearing his throat he replied, "Nothing."

"I like your braids." She complimented.

"You do?"

"Yeah I do."

She acted like she was trying to get him to say

more. He licked his lips and teased his chin. Mike tried to be cool as he pumped himself up before telling her, "Thanks. Can I tell you something?" "Yeah sure, what's up?" "I've been wanting to holla at you for a minute, but hell, my nerves are bad."

"They don't seem bad now." When she said that he hesitated. He stared like he did many times before. She then said, "What's wrong? Why you staring like that? That's a little creepy."

He figured at that point to just go for it. Mike then spoke, "I'm probably tripping for asking you this, but oh well. When we gonna you know, get it in?" As soon as those words left his lips, he realized those were the dumbest words he had ever said to her. He didn't know what she was thinking as she looked at him with those hypnotizing gray eyes.

She blew him away when she replied, "Oh, that's how you feel?" Mike was still frozen and she knew she had caught him off guard. She then said, "Aren't we getting ahead of ourselves?"

He continued to amp himself up, it was either now or never. Licking his lips again and rubbing his hands together, he said, "True, but I've been holding back my feelings about a lot of things lately and honestly, it's eating me up. I haven't felt like myself as of late, but if you aren't down, I understand, it's cool. I just think you beautiful as hell. I don't want to pass up the opportunity of having someone like you in my life."

Lida did not say a word as she considered his offer. It was about time he spoke up. Mike began to feel embarrassed when she didn't respond. In all truth, he was still a virgin and had no idea what sex would be like but everybody made it seem like it was what you did when you were truly in love with someone. Little did he know, Lida was flattered and felt the same way he did. She had already made up her mind to get with him, and Mike speaking his mind sealed the deal.

She then said, "Well you are cute and you did catch me off guard with that, but why don't we start out slow. Why don't you take me out to the movies one of these weekends? When you do that, we can go from there and see what happens."

"Cool, why don't you give me your number so I can call you."

"Ok that's cool, just hit me up." Mike fidgeted in his pockets for something to write on. When he finally found something he handed it to her and she wrote it down. She ran her fingers down his chest, and spoke before walking away, "Later baby."

"Alight later." Mike said. He felt like L. L. Cool J as he walked away tucking the paper in his pocket.

As he made it to the door he remembered what he had actually come there for. He turned back and went to pick up his check. Feeling accomplished, he went and put some money in his bank account, and then hit the mall.

CHAPTER 4

Almost a month had past and Mina was Mike's primary concern. The incident with Carlos was behind and his mother's recovery was remarkable, she would be going home soon. His brother and sister hadn't talked to their father and they didn't want to. Mike was still holding up strong. He and Cali were tight, kicking it whenever he had free time. It felt good to be around another guy for a change.

Mike eventually called Lida and made a date. Going out with her was all he could think about. Mike was anxious, he just wanted to make a good first impression. He wondered what had he gotten himself into as the Friday came. Lida told him she would be by at eight, but it was half an hour past that. He told her specifically to meet him at Jean's house because Jean wanted to meet her. He was using Jean's car so he offered to pick her up but she said she had running around to do with her grandmother.

Jean was a good judge of character and he talked about Lida constantly, that made Jean want to meet her even more. With her being late, he began to think she was playing him and if she was, he didn't know how he would handle it.

'I wish mama was here, she would tell me

what to do,' he thought. When the doorbell rang his heart began to beat rapidly. Making sure he saw her first, he yelled out, "I got it." When his hand touched the doorknob, he wanted to throw up again. Trying to calm down, he opened the door and the first thing he said was, "Oh God, you are so beautiful."

She gave him that smile he loved and replied, "Thank you." She stood there as Mike stared and took in her beauty. "You going to let me in or do I have to stay out here all night?" Lida asked.

Realizing that she was still outside he blushed and said, "I'm sorry. Yea, yea beautiful, please come on in."

He moved out the way and let her in. When he closed the door, Lida said, "Sorry I am late. I had to wait for my grandmother to finish up, we've been running around all day. She also said to tell your grandmother hi."

"I hope you don't mind, but my grandmother wants to meet you anyway."

"Naw you good."

She grabbed Mike's hand and let him lead her to the living room. Lida thought it was cute for him to be so nervous. Mike being himself was one reason she liked him. He was so different when he wasn't pretending to be hard. Mike showed her to the couch and offered her a seat. He called out for Jean, and she came into the living room. He hoped their meeting would go well. When his grandmother entered the room, Lida stood up and smiled. Jean walked over to her and Mike said, "Grandma, this is Lida and Lida, this is my grandma Jean."

Lida held out her hand, but Jean bypassed it and gave her a warm hug. Lida smiled bigger, it had been a while since she had felt a hug that welcoming. Releasing her, Jean said, "Hey baby. It is so nice to meet you."

"It is nice to meet you as well ma'am, and my grandmother told me to tell you hi."

"Tell her hi and I send her my blessings."

"I sure will."

"Mike has told me so much about you. Everything he told me really did you no justice. You are so beautiful and well mannered."

"Thank you."

"No, thank you baby."

Jean looked at Mike and asked, "Leave us girls alone for a few minutes please!? I promise I won't make you late."

"Yes ma'am."

Mike was starting to regret having Lida meet him there. He had been waiting on the date since the first day he saw her, and now his grandmother was hogging up his time with her. He tried to eavesdrop on their conversation and prayed she didn't bring out the baby pictures. Jean turned to Lida and said, "So Lida, how have you been doing?"

"Oh, I've been doing fine. Thank you for asking."

"You're welcome. How has your grandmother been doing these days?"

"She has been doing better since the surgery. Now she is back to work and hasn't missed a beat."

"That's good to hear." Mike wondered why Jean was talking so low. He continued to listen, but he could barely hear them. "I am going to get to the point as to why I wanted to talk to you."

"Ok."

"Mike has seen his share of pain over these last few months with my daughter and her boyfriend. I know you are a couple years older than he is and I want to make sure you know what you're dealing with."

"Ok," Lida said nervously.

"I don't want my grandson to get hurt, but I

also don't want him to hurt anyone, he doesn't always express his feelings well."

Lida understood where Jean was coming from, so it wasn't a problem. "Yes ma'am. He has been acting different lately. I want to say angry, but I don't know. I see him with other people and he just looks mad but when he is with me he's a different person. The same thing happened to my brother when our mom died last year. I was the same way. I hope I can help Mike in some way because I understand how he feels."

"Try to get him to open up for me. I know he probably hasn't told you about his mother, has he?"

"No, he has not, but I can try and talk to him about it."

"I know he'll talk to you."

"I will do my best."

"Great. Well I know he is freaking out and wondering what we are talking about." They both stood up as Jean called out, "Mike your date is ready." She turned back to Lida and said, "It was great talking to you and thank you.

It was a pleasure to finally meet you, and thank you so much Lida."

Mike walked in the room trying to judge the

atmosphere. He looked at Lida and asked, "You ready?"

"Yes I am." She said smiling.

He looked back at Jean and said, "I will see you in a few hours grandma, love you."

"You two be careful and I love you too."

Jean kissed her grandson on the forehead. They left out the house and Mike tried to recall all of the do's and don'ts that Mina taught him when taking a girl out. He opened the door for her. She said thank you as he closed it when she got in. Getting inside, he locked down and cranked the car up.

Wanting to know what all she said because he could not hear that well, he asked, "I want to apologize on how she cornered you like that."

"It's no problem."

"So what all did you and my grandma talk about?"

"Not much. She kind of reminds me of my grandmother."

"She does?"

"Yeah, she does."

"I also wanted to say sorry for coming at you

like I did at work that day. I meant it, but I might had been kind of rude."

"Yeah I know, but I am glad you got up the nerve to talk to me. Tiny has been telling me all the things you been saying, and I was just sitting and waiting on you to say something to me." Mike drove a few more miles and hoped Tiny didn't say anything to embarrass him. Lida noticed how he clammed up again. She then asked, "How is your mom? Your grandmother told me she is in the hospital."

"Yeah, she's doing better now."

"What happened?"

He wasn't ready to talk about it. Playing it off, he stated, "It's a long story, but she will be home next week. Things have been crazy, that's what I mean."

In a comforting tone, Lida said softly as she caressed his cheek and played in his hair, "I can understand that."

Swallowing hard, he replied, "Thanks! I appreciate that."

Although on the inside he was crying and desired to tell her, he felt she wouldn't understand. They went inside the movies and the whole time Mike could not think straight. He paid no attention to the movie. His every thought was on Lida and how much he really liked her. A few times, she felt him look at her and he even convinced himself to put his arm around her shoulder. Lida welcomed it as she leaned in and placed her head on his shoulder. That made Lida smile. Mike treated her like a jewel and she appreciated every bit of it.

When the movie was over, they decided to walk downtown along the peer near the beach. Mike reached for her hand and she didn't hesitate to give it to him. The sound of the water and the smell of the air brought back memories. He then said, "I always liked coming down here to think. It is so peaceful."

"Yea it is." She agreed.

"My mom used to bring me down here all the time when we lived in the projects. It's funny how being so young, you think your parents have it all figured out. I used to catch her crying and smiling at the same time. I thought it would be rude to ask her what was wrong, so I kept quiet but she was always at peace when we came here."

Lida continued to listen as they walked. The way she paid attention to him meant the world to him. He was in his special place with a special girl. It couldn't get any better than that. "I've never been this far down. I had no idea how nice and peaceful this is." Lida said admiring the lights on the pier.

"You still come out here a lot?"

When she said that, they came upon some stairs where they stopped and sat down. Mike said, "I do because when I'm here it feels like nothing can get to me and whatever is bothering me, doesn't matter anymore."

Lida turned and looked at Mike as the wind blowing, was making his eyes water. Still holding his hand she asked "Are you and your mom still close? The way you talk I can tell you really care about her."

"We used to be like best friends. I would tell her everything, but lately we don't really talk much. I mean I go see her every other day but it's nothing like it used to be. Her boyfriend is the main reason we grew apart."

"Is he the reason why she in the hospital?"

Suddenly he exploded on Lida. He jerked his hand away and stood up with bitterness and anger. "God, you nosey!"

Lida continued to sit on the steps looking up at him as she replied, "Huh?"

"You don't know nothing about me!"

Lida was stunned. Things were going so great. He was opening up and letting her into his world. Without warning, he flipped on her and she didn't understand why. Just to let him know she was not the one to be yelled at, Lida stood up on the next to the last step so she could get in his face.

Staring into his eyes snapping back she replied, "First of all don't talk to me like that. I'm not one of those lame hoes that you deal with every day. I was trying to talk to you because I felt what you were saying. If you are going to act like that don't even talk to me, take me home!"

Mike knew right then that he had messed up. Tears were forcing their way down his cheek as he replied, "Lida, I am so sorry for popping off like that. I don't usually tell people this stuff, you got me feeling vulnerable as hell. My mama is the only one I talk to about this kind of stuff. I'm just hurting and I don't know what to do."

Lida was falling for him. She knew it because a tear formed in the corner of her eye. The more his tears appeared, the more she wiped them away. Being a female, she knew how to handle this situation. She tenderly spoke to him, "Believe it or not Mike, I know how you feel. When my mom died last year, a part of me was lost. I know your mom's not dead, but I know the pain you are feeling. You have to believe I am not here to hurt you. You can trust me baby."

He gave a slight grin as she kissed his forehead, then his lips. Mike reached up and gave her a hug. His transparency touched her soul. He didn't want to let go of her and she wasn't letting him go. When the moment was over, they walked back to the car.

Mike was grateful for Lida. The whole night she didn't offer any opinions and she didn't judge. She only listened. He was amazed at how easy it was to talk to her. At the end of the night, Mike had to force himself to take her home. He didn't want the night to end. Truthfully they both wanted the night to go on, but Lida had to go home and he had to return the car. When they made it to her house, he got out and opened her door. He gently touched the small of her back as he walked her to the front door.

He glanced toward Lida and saw that she was staring at him this time. It was odd to have her look at him that way. He stopped at the door and asked her, "Why are you looking at me like that?"

"I was just wondering what is going through your head right now?"

"Truthfully, I want to kiss you."

"Well do it."

He leaned into her for the kiss, but paused short of her lips to say, "Naw, not yet. The time is not right." Lida didn't know what to do or think. He smelled so good as they stood pelvis' touching. She wanted him right then and right there. Why wouldn't he complete the evening with a kiss? Chills and goose bumps covered her arms and a chill went down her spine as he kissed her on the neck. Mike leaned back up with a smirk and told her "I just want tonight to continue the next time I see you. I hope that's ok?"

Lida gave him a, 'You think you smart,' grin. Mike smiled. She then said, "Mike you think you are slick, don't you?"

"What? Naw I'm not trying to be slick. Me? How?"

"You get me turned on and wet just to say, continue next time we see each other? Let me go in the house before you try something else."

Mike was shocked but proud. But that wasn't what he was trying to do. Mina had told him not to ever rush things because they would happen in their own time, with the right girl. Mike found that he liked that advice she gave him, it worked better than he expected. He ended the night saying, "I had a good time with you tonight and I would love to do this again."

Lida with a smile responded, "Ha-ha, good time huh? Ok."

Mike's confidence was now to the roof. He grabbed her hand and said, "We will do this again. I will call you tomorrow."

"Bye baby."

Mike turned her hand over and kissed it tenderly. She gave him a smile of approval as he walked back to his car. Lida went in the house and Mike drove off toward Jean's. This was priceless, the night couldn't have gone any better. When he made it back home, he told Jean all about his night with Lida. Jean smiled and told him how happy she was for him. He even told Shawn and Nika about his night. Of course they laughed at him and teased saying he was sprung.

CHAPTER 5

Mike was on his way to see Mina. As soon as he made it to her room, he was appalled by what he saw. Walking out of his mother's room was Carlos. Seeing that man leaving out of his mother's room brought back those emotions he was trying to let go of. Carlos saw Mike and didn't say anything to him. They made eye contact as they kept walking. The first question Mike asked Mina was, "How did he get out?" He followed up asking, "What is Carlos doing coming out of your room?"

Having the feeling he would not understand, she only replied, "He just wanted to talk. He brought me flowers and said he was sorry. Mostly he was just making promises that everything is going to be different when I come home. Carlos said we all will be a real family, just the way I always wanted it."

Mike continued to stand there staring at his mother. He could not believe what she was saying. With a dumbfounded look he had to ask, "Are you serious? This fool put you in the hospital, in a coma at that. After all this time, he has the nerves to show up with flowers, promises and oh yeah, an apology, and everything is supposed to be ok now? Mama that's bogus." Mina did not say anything. She knew how angry her son was, so she just laid there and watched him pace up and down the floor saying over and over again, "This is crazy!"

Mike briefly forgot who he was talking to. Mina sat up in the bed and said, "Boy you better calm down. Now sit down in this chair next to me."

Reluctantly he obeyed, but found it hard to keep still. He looked at her and said, "Mama, it doesn't make any sense for you to just forgive him like that. What about us? What about your children?" Mina saw the concern upon his face as the tears began to form. The tears weren't because he was sad, but the longer he sat there the more enraged he became. Mike pounded into his hand with his fist. She then heard him say, "I swear if he touches you again I'm going to kill him. You better trust what I say mama." For years Mina tried to teach him how to control his anger, but when it involved someone he cared about he would be hard to contain. Mina glanced at her son and he said when he stood up, "That is nonsense! I'm old enough to know love when I see it and that ain't it. If you going to bring him back to the house, I'm not going to be there!"

When he stormed out the room, he heard Mina calling after him. He did not care, he kept walking. When he made it to the lobby, the room started spinning out of control. Visions of him doing horrible things to Carlos flashed before him. His anger was consuming him.

67

He went outside to get some air. As he stood in the parking lot he closed his eyes and tried to calm himself. Sighing in despair, he knew as much as he loved his family, if Carlos was coming back, he was not going to be there. Mike meant it and he wasn't going to have it any other way.

He slammed the door of Jean's house. His attitude was in full affect. Cutting him off was Jean. She snatched him by the arm and said, "Michael I can see that you are mad, but you need to calm down and talk to me."

"Grandma I need to be alone right now, please let me go."

Jean spoke carefully, "Ok I know something probably has you wanting to scream, but sooner or later, you're going to have to let it out. Isolating yourself from those that love you is not the answer."

He didn't say anything else as he heard Shawn and Nika in the hallway trying to figure out what was wrong with him. Mike stormed off to his room and closed the door behind him. Once the door was shut, everybody knew to leave him alone.

Shortly afterward Lida called. Jean had spoken to her while Mike was gone and had told her to come over. Lida was calling to see if he was back. A half an hour later, she pulled up in her grandmother's car. Minutes later a soft knock was heard at Mike's door.

He didn't feel like talking and didn't care who it was until he heard, "Mike it's me, Lida."

His head perked up at hearing her voice. She was the only person he did want to see. What he was going through wasn't her fault and he wasn't going to take anything out on her. For her to be at his bedroom door, he knew his grandmother must have called her, because company was not allowed past the bathroom. Taking his time, he opened the door.

"Baby what's wrong? What has happened?"

He stood there with a headache and bloodshot eyes from crying. Mike stood to the side for her to come in. He left the door open and motioned for her to sit on the bed. She did as he asked and he sat down beside her. "Lida I'm losing it. My mama just told me that she is getting back with her boyfriend when she gets out. I didn't think she would do it, but I saw him today at the hospital leaving out of her room. Why would she do that? Why would she place us and herself back in danger like that?"

"Mike, I am going to be honest with you. Women do crazy things when they are in love or want to be loved, even if the one they love has hurt them. Don't hate her for wanting to be loved. The truth is, you can't be responsible for her actions or choices."

The way she brought it to him made sense. He didn't like it, but it made sense. Lida touched his face, and he spoke, "As long as my grandma lets me stay here, I will. I refuse to go back and I mean it."

"I understand."

Lida gave Mike the warmest hug he had felt in a very long time. Even as she told him she understood he believed her. He was glad she was there for him because his heart begged her not to let him go. She didn't.

Moments later, Mike heard Jean walk past the room to look in on them. His ears followed her footsteps as they headed toward Shawn and Nika's room. Muffled voices were heard as Jean told them about the situation. He hoped that they knew he wasn't mad at them because he knew they were in a tough predicament. Giving his attention back to Lida, he smiled. She was there for him and only she was able to give him any hint of hope.

Lida left a little while later and he hated to see her go, but her grandmother had to go to work. Mike decided to take the time to be alone and gather his thoughts and figure out his next move. Exhausted from the day's events he fell into a deep sleep not even waking for dinner.

The following day, Mina left the hospital heading home. Mike didn't go. He didn't think he could stomach her or her choice. However, Shawn and Nika prepared to go back home because Carlos had insisted they be with him. The summer was also wrapping up and school was about to start. He had no idea how he was going to handle being a senior and being alone, for that matter.

The next day Mike called Cali to come pick him up, he was off from work and needed to get out of the house. While they rolled down the Boulevard, they stopped at JoJo's to grab something to eat. While they stood and waited for their food Cali said, "Aye man, check this out. You know I got love for you right? And I know it ain't my place to be speaking on your relationship and all but I think you need to watch that chick Lida." Mike wasn't expecting that. He wondered where all of this was coming from.

"Why you say that? What she do to you?"

"Nothing man, it's her whole character, there's just something off about her. I'm just saying watch yourself."

"I guess man, I mean I admit she doesn't like me hanging with you but that's as far as it goes."

"Mike look, when it comes to matters of the heart, you must tread lightly. I'm just being straight up with you and man to man, she ain't the one for you."

71

"I hear you."

"That's just me though, you do what you want. I got your back either way. I know she has you wide open, but be careful. I been in the game a long time and I have dealt with broads like her before."

"I hope you wrong Cali. I hope you wrong."

"Me too bro."

A few days passed and Mike began to notice things becoming distant between he and Lida, since Cali had begun to hang around more. Mike had hoped that things would get back to normal for them, but didn't think on it too long. He thought about the conversation with Cali and he knew without a doubt that Cali was real. On the other hand, so was Lida. She was a woman, just like his mother. Just thinking about it reminded him that he hadn't seen her since she went home. Mike called Cali and asked him to give him a ride to go see Mina. He would have walked but it had been raining all day.

When Cali answered the phone he said, "What's up lil' bro?"

"Nothing right now, but I need to know if you can take me to see my mom? My grandma said I need to go see her. I don't know what for though. If she was so concerned, why hasn't she been over here to see me? Nobody has questioned that."

To Mike it didn't make a difference to him which way the wind blew at this point. Cali voiced his opinion by saying, "True, but she is moms. Just tell her you were just stopping by to check on her. Anyway, I will be there in a few."

When Cali pulled up like he said he would, Mike told his grandmother that he would be back in a few. As Mike walked toward the car, he was kind of nervous. He and his mom hadn't spoken in so long but he knew he needed to see if she was okay.

Mike got in and they spoke. Cali turned the radio up as they pulled off. They rode without speaking for a few. Mike was gathering his thoughts and seeing that he looked to be in deep thought, Cali respected it. The closer they got to Mina's, Mike got nervous all over again. He had no idea what he was going to say. Cali looked over at Mike and said over the radio "Aye look in the glove compartment, I got something for you." Mike was curious and the smirk on Cali's face didn't make it any better. He opened it and saw a brown bag tucked inside. He looked over at Cali who nodded for him to take the bag out. Inside was a black and grey compact 9 mm. "You know how to use one of those?" Cali said grinning. "Yea, I appreciate this man." "Ain't nothing, like I told you before, if you going to be out here you can't be naked. Consider it as a gift, just make sure not to pull it out unless you intend on using it. We don't do warning shots around here." Mike nodded in agreement and tucked the pistol in his waistline.

Mike turned the radio down as they approached the house because he knew Mina didn't like loud music. He didn't want her tripping before he even got in the house. Cali looked at him and smiled. He parked his car in the alley near the house. Mike sat there for a few minutes.

"You want to come in?"

Cali would have preferred not to but he didn't like the idea of sitting in that alley, so he replied jokingly. "Yeah man, I ain't about to sit out here like a duck. I'm asking to get jacked or something."

They laughed as they got out the car. Taking his time, Mike walked slowly towards the sidewalk. When they made it to the front door, he knocked and Mina yelled out, "Come in!"

Mike opened the door and noticed the house still looked the same, only brighter. It still had that clean, motherly smell to it and that gave him a reason to smile. When he didn't see her, he figured she was in the kitchen. Making his way through the living room to the kitchen, he saw her sitting at the table with a stack of bills, a lit cigarette and a glass of brandy. She looked up at him and smiled.

Mike smiled back and said, "Hey mama, how you doing?"

She extended her arms wincing in pain and spoke with nervous sounds. "Come here baby and give me a hug."

Although it was awkward, he did as she asked. When he pulled back from her she said, "You look exhausted. Have you been getting any sleep?"

"Yeah I'm good mama, just been working." As she sat back down, Mina glanced over at Cali and blew out a puff of smoke. Mike noticed and said, "I'm sorry mama, this is my friend Cali, Cali this is my mama Mina." They exchanged greetings and Cali stood at the door. Mike sat down at the table with her, and confessed, "I would have been here sooner, but I wasn't sure if Carlos would be around. I am not in the mood to be around him right now."

Mike hung his head some and began tapping his house key on the table. Mina softly said, "Baby don't worry about that. I'll take care of that." Again she looked over at Cali. He nodded. With his head down Mike did not notice the interaction between them. "You just make sure you take care of yourself. You're a man now and there isn't much I can say to you at this point but to be careful, snakes are out there."

Mike noticed when she said that, she was turning her head away from Cali. Seeing the look on Mike's face, Cali said, "Awe Ms. Henderson, I ain't gonna let nothing happen to him. Mike is like a little brother to me. I got him."

Mina had no idea how serious Cali was about defending Mike. Her son was like a brother to him and he would kill anyone that came at Mike the wrong way. He and Mike had become just that tight.

Mina took another drag of her cigarette letting out a harsh cough. Breaking the tense air, Mike asked, "Mama what's up with all these bills? Carlos not helping you? Matter of fact I still want to know how in hell did he get out?"

"He bonded out and his lawyer found a loop hole in the robbery case and it got thrown out. He has nine lives I swear. And don't worry about those bills. You know I always figure something out."

"Still mama, there is no reason for the bills to be unpaid. I worked all summer to help out around here and I know I gave you enough money to help cover everything. Where did the money go?" Mina was silent. She knew he would hit the roof if he knew she loaned Carlos the money. Before she could finally answer him he said, "You gave the money to Carlos didn't you? Mama I'm not stupid. I'm going to kill that fool!"

Mina couldn't compose herself any longer, although it had been some time since they had spoken she didn't like the tone he was taking with her. The

West Indian in her rose up. She jumped up and grabbed him by his collar. "You listen to me Michael Henderson, I am still your mother and you will respect me. I know you may not agree with my choices but they are my choices. You watch how you talk to me!" Mike snatched away and stood two feet away from his mother. Mina feared her son for the first time. She had never seen him so full of rage. Trying to back him down she scoffed, "You are most definitely your father's son! Look, I know you are angry, but being angry won't get you anywhere but in trouble!" Mina poked her finger in his chest to say, "I am still your mother, like it or not!"

Mike feeling vindicated, snatched her hand away from him and stepped closer to his mother. They were face to face, and Cali seeing it about to get out of hand, got between them and said to his friend, "Mike man, chill out. That's moms. We can take care of the other thing later, but this ain't you. Apologize right now."

Mike hesitated but it was an O.G. call and he had to respect Cali at that point. He let out a sigh and as much as he didn't want to he moved back a few paces. He mumbled the words, "I'm sorry."

Mina didn't say a word as her son sat back down. Seeing that, gave her a new respect for Cali. Mina finally said, "Baby you are just mad right now, just trust me I got this."

Mike didn't say anything more. Mina looked at Cali and asked, "Can you take him and help him calm down some more?"

"Yes ma'am I can." Cali turned toward Mike and said, "Bro go wait in the car, I will be there in a minute. I want to talk to your moms real quick." Mike silently got up and left out of the house. When the door closed, Cali said to Mina, "I am not going to let anything happen to Mike. As for Carlos, don't worry about him, I told you I would take care of that for you."

Mina took a sip of her drink and asked, "You didn't tell him did you?"

"No I didn't. You said don't say anything so I didn't." What Mike didn't know was that even though Cali always said he was like his little brother there was actually some truth to it. Cali was also known as Calmese, which was his father's Chaos' real name. Mina had wanted to tell him but when things blew up with Carlos, she didn't feel it would ever be the right time. Cali had heard that Mina was in the hospital from his girlfriend who was a nurse there. It wasn't a coincidence that Cali just happened to be there weeks ago when Mike was getting jumped. After Cali came by to see Mina at the hospital she had him watching after Mike the whole time. "Thank you, when the time is right I will tell him. He just has so much anger inside him I don't want to lose my baby forever."

Cali reached inside his pocket and pulled out an envelope containing five thousand dollars. Mina pushed his hand away, but Cali gave it to her anyway. "You don't have to do this. I always figure something out."

"No take it. I told you he is my little brother, so when he's hurting, I'm hurting. That makes you my mama too, so I got you."

Mina sighed and nodded in agreement to say, "Just watch after him, you hear?"

Cali left and in her heart Mina released Mike and could only pray he would be alright. When Cali went to the car, he didn't mention anything about the money. He just assured Mike that things would be alright and asked for him to trust him on it.

There was no question that Mike trusted Cali. The ride back to Jean's house was quiet. Before Mike opened the door, Cali turned to him and spoke with concern, "Man you like my lil' brother so I'm going to look after you, you know what I'm saying? But you have to chill out talking to your mom like that. I know it's messed up, but she is still moms. She's going to be alright."

Mike knew Cali was right, so he didn't argue. He just nodded before saying, "I feel ya bro. It's just crazy right now and I don't like feeling like this. Trust is an issue for me and I'm going to protect me and mine."

Cali's said, "I got you, so don't worry about nothing."

"Cali man, I appreciate you looking out for me. I know you have my best interest at heart, even when I don't. Thank you man."

"Aye that's what big bros do. Just be cool. I will hit you up this weekend. I got some things to take care of."

"Ok get at me then."

"Bet."

Mike got out the car and went into the house and up to his room. Once there, he thought about everything that had transpired with Mina and he still had no idea how much he was going to be able to take.

CHAPTER 6

The more he thought about Cali's words, the more he thought about her. He didn't think it was fair, but to him, life was not fair. It had been days since he seen or talked to Lida. He needed to know if they were still okay.

It was a Friday and he made up his mind to walk over to Lida's house. As he got closer to her house, he saw a bunch of cars and had a feeling that something was not right. Then he remembered Lida's brother along with some other family was supposed to be in town from Louisiana. Her brother Corey never could stand Michigan City which was why he only stayed one summer before moving back home. Her family was having a dinner for her grandmother's birthday.

He figured he probably shouldn't be there. He thought that what he was going through would bring her mood down. Deciding to turn around, he turned and began to walk back the way he had come. In the midst of him thinking to himself, he heard, "Mikey! Mikey!" He turned to see that it was Lida. He stopped as she walked toward him in a light jog to catch up to him and asked, "What's up?"

"Nothing, I was coming to see you, but I can come by later when you are free."

He didn't really want to be around her family. The look on her face made him feel like a coward because at that point, he noticed that he was always leaving her hanging. She grabbed his hand so he couldn't walk off. "Wait! Please don't go. I don't want to go back in there without you with me."

He faced her and placed his arm around her and asked, "What's wrong?"

"I just don't fit in with them anymore and without my mom being here I don't really want to be around them. I only feel comfortable with you, my brother and my grandmother. I just need you to be here."

Her look of desperation left no other need for words. Mike followed Lida back to her house. He saw how she could feel uncomfortable as she led him through the house full of people back to her room. Mike stood at the door, not really wanting to go in.

"What is it?"

"Lida, I've never been in a girl's room before."

"Boy come in here and quit playing."

As he took inventory of her room, he was surprised by how simple it was. Pictures of her mom were all around and it smelled like peaches. Nothing was out of place. She touched the bed beside her and said, "You won't get in trouble, come sit down. I'm not going to bite, just don't put your feet on my bed."

As he continued to investigate the room at the head of the bed he saw a diary sticking from under her pillow. He reached for it, and Lida looked at him diving across the bed rolling off the other side. Panting and laughing, she looked at him and said "Boy why you so nosey?"

Mike thought her being protective was too funny. Sitting back down he looked at her, smiled and said, "I wasn't going to read it, but if you love me, you would let me read it."

He knew he went left field with that one. He was testing her to see if she felt the same way he did. He refused to be the first one to say "I love you." He had an insecure look on his face as he waited to see what her response would be. She sat close to him and held his hand, "Why is it so hard for you to believe somebody loves you? Haven't you figured out how I feel?"

"Ha-ha, don't play with me."

"I'm not playing Mikey."

She handed him the diary and said "Does that answer your question?" No woman besides his mother and grandmother had ever said they loved him before. He was stumped and didn't know how to answer. He thought of every reason he could, but found none. His heart raced and his stomach knotted up. Lida leaned over and kissed him seductively.

Mike was confused as he tasted the strawberry flavor lip gloss. Muscles tensed in unusual places as his racing heart forced his blood to pump faster. He wasn't sure what she expected him to do next so he kissed her back. Within a few minutes, Mike felt himself being aroused. If he wasn't any good this could all go bad. He didn't want sex to mess things up with her. Lida meant too much to him. All doubt raced through his mind and he convinced himself not to go any further. He could hear Jean's voice in his head say, "You can't make your mind do what your heart can't." It was then that he knew he actually loved Lida.

He pulled himself together and said in a low voice, "I can't, we…we can't do this. Baby I want to make love to you but I don't want to mess things up between us. I hope you understand?"

Lida being filled with passion and her hormones raging didn't want to hear that. She couldn't wait for Mike to take her. But as she saw the sincerity in his eyes she came to her senses. She stared at him with confusion and appreciation, but feeling slightly rejected. Taking a deep breath, Lida let it out saying, "Wow! I don't know what to say. No one has ever made me feel this important. Mikey I love you so much. Come with me for a second." She took his hand and led him out of the room back through the kitchen. Confused, Mike followed her to the deck out back where it was quieter. He sat down on a chair and she sat on his lap. Lida played with his braids and stared into his eyes. When he looked up, a tear teetered on her eyelash. He took the top of his index finger and caught it before it could drop.

"You know something Mikey, when I was young, I prayed for someone like you."

"How so?"

"I had prayed for someone just like my dad."

"Wow really? And what kind of person was he?"

"Someone that believed in family and was actually willing to love me without asking me to do something I didn't want to do. Someone that I could count on when everyone else let me down."

Mike had no response to that. He had always blamed God for everything that had happened in his life, but he was beginning to rethink his position, the more they talked. Before he realized it, three hours passed them by and people were starting to leave.

"What time is it?"

"About eleven thirty."

"Awe man I have to go. I don't want my grandma worrying about me. I don't want to go, but you know how it is. Give me a hug."

Lida stood up and gave Mike a long hug and a kiss. When they released the embrace, they walked hand in hand to the front of the house.

"No one has ever gotten this close to me. There is something about you that I can't explain."

"I feel the same way. It's like all my life I had been waiting for you and here you are. But now, you have to go and I won't keep you. I can't wait till we get to spend more time together."

"I know, me either."

"How about we meet back up tomorrow night?"

"That's fine, but call me when you get home, ok?"

"Ok."

"I love you Mikey."

"I love you too."

Those words coming from her put a huge smile on his face. He went home happier than ever.

The next morning as soon as the sun brightened the day, Mike and Shawn went to the park to play basketball. It was nice to get out and spend time with his brother. He wasn't thinking about anything negative. He was in a good space. He spent all morning with his brother and he couldn't remember the last time he enjoyed himself that much.

When they returned to Jean's house, the duo saw her sitting at the kitchen table peeling sweet potatoes for dinner. Shawn went around back as she called Mike inside. "Sit down and let's talk." He knew it had to be something serious from the way her words lingered after him. Being obedient, he sat down and watched her as she continued peeling. Without stopping to look up Jean asked, "So you ready to tell me about how things went with your mama?"

He wanted to downplay it but couldn't lie to her, so he said, "Grandma, I'm going to be honest. Things seemed different. It was like I didn't even know her anymore and it hurts. If it weren't for Cali and Lida being there for me, I don't know what I would do."

"I know it must be tough, but I know my daughter. She is only doing what she thinks is best for you."

"How can she when she goes back to him?"

Mike countered. "It doesn't matter what he does, she still goes back to him. Can she not see that he is not right for her?"

"Mike, love is different for everybody. She loves Carlos, even if we don't see why. She can leave him and go about her business, but she will still love him. She may even be miserable without him, but she would rather be happy. If Carlos does that for her, there is nothing we can say or do about it!"

"Grandma that may be true, but does all love have to be like that?"

"No, only God given love can change the way people think and feel. It is only through his love that we can understand the unexplainable."

Mike thought about it for a minute, his grandmother was telling the truth. He knew she was making sure he didn't burn any bridges he may have to cross later. Being truthful he replied, "To be honest grandma, I don't think I've ever been this happy before in my life. At the same time I haven't been so sad either." His grandmother looked confused, so he said, "Things with Lida are still cool and seem to be getting better. I just hope I don't mess it up."

"Baby I know. Just be yourself. Do right by her and be honest about how you feel. If you are not honest with yourself, how can you think others will be honest with you?"

"I don't know grandma."

Mike gave his grandmother a peck on the cheek and went up to his room. He got on the phone and called Lida. On the first ring she answered, "Hello."

"Hey Lida."

"Hey baby, how's it going? You still coming to the church with me tonight?"

"Huh, church?" Mike had no idea what she was talking about.

"Remember I told you about it a couple weeks ago? Don't tell me you forgot?" In the midst of their time apart Mike had totally forgotten that he had agreed to go to church with Lida and her grandmother. Trying to save face he said, "Oh yeah, I'm trippin'. Yeah we good, I'll be there."

"Ok, so anyway how you doing?"

"Great, kind of nervous about this whole revival thing, you know how I feel about this stuff."

"Mikey, there's nothing to be nervous about."

"Easy for you to say."

"Maybe. I think you are going to enjoy yourself."

"How you going to think that at a revival? Enjoy and revival don't go together."

Lida laughed as she spoke, "The usual pastor is not speaking. A visiting preacher is doing it."

"Oh."

"Do that give you comfort?"

"A little. I don't know, I guess."

"Mikey, I am going to be by your side the whole time. Stop worrying."

He replied, "That makes me a little comfortable I guess. So…"

Lida interrupted "Baby I have to get off of here. Grandma has a call coming in, I'll call you tonight when it's time to go. Alright?"

"Ok."

"I love you Mikey."

"Love you too."

They both hung up. Mike looked forward to spending time with Lida more than he did being around a bunch of church folks. Normally, he would be against it, but decided why not as long as he got a chance to be with Lida.

That night when they got to church, he was quickly reminded why he hadn't been to church since he was nine. It all was so unreal. As they walked through the parking lot, ringing in their ears was the sound of tambourines, drums and an organ with people clapping and shouting. The closer he got to the front door, the more he regretted letting her talk him into going. Before they opened the door, he asked silently and nervously, "Are you sure about this? I don't know what to do when I get in there."

"Don't worry baby, just be yourself. It'll be fine."

"I don't know Lida."

"Baby I am here with you. Don't be nervous. I got you."

That was the second time that day he had heard, 'Just be yourself.' He had no idea how to do that in a church. Lida opened the door. Mike shook as his head and his stomach did that thing again. His first thought was to not go pass the last pew in the back, but her grandmother led them all the way to the front.

Once they took their seats, the music slowed down and the entire church started to get quiet. A tall, scary looking man came forth. Mike took it that he was the preacher Lida told him about when he went to the podium. In a deep baritone voice, he spoke,

"Good evening family. Isn't God good? Before we go any further, I feel a heaviness in my spirit. There is something I must say. I don't know who it is for, but the Lord has assured me that they will know what I am talking about and who I'm talking to."

Out of nowhere, Mike became anxious and felt that the people were looking at him. He even began to beg the Lord to not let the preacher look at him. He knew that if that happened, he was running out and not going back.

"Thus says the Lord. I know you don't believe that I care about you and what you are going through. I know you think I've been ignoring you lately, but my child, it is not true. I desire to change your situation and to change you too. You've suffered a lot and I've been with you through it all."

Mike's eyes started to well with water and he did all he could to stop the flow of tears. To him, it didn't feel like God was there. He just could not believe God cared about him or his life. But what if he was wrong? What if everything was just to get him to the point where he was now? Then the preacher spoke, "It's time for you to come out, but first, you must forgive. I need you to forgive Me for it was My will for you to endure what you have in order to bring you here now. I love you more than you will ever know. Let me show you just how much." The preacher stepped down from the pulpit,

92

walked in front of the church and scanned the audience. Clearing his throat he said, "I believe the person the message is for knows it was for them, and I just want to assure you that God never lies. He loves you just that much. Now is your chance to be free, come forward now. Listen to the voice in your heart urging you to believe. So come."

At that very second, tears raced down his face. As much as he wanted them to stop, he couldn't. It was an emotional overload for him as his body began to tingle all over. He could not stay still, as hard as he tried to stay seated it seemed his body had other plans. Suddenly he got the urge to stand. He paused briefly then stood up. Lida grabbed his hand. He glanced down at her and noticed she was crying as well with a huge smile on her face. The preacher walked over to Mike and did not say a word. No words were needed the preacher just hugged him. Mike could not help but to cry and wonder why God allowed Mina to suffer so much over and over again. What did he do that would make her choose Carlos over her flesh and blood? Those were the questions he wanted to ask God.

No one could hear as the preacher whispered in his ear, "My son, can you forgive?"

Mike looked at him and nodded. But he didn't know how. He prayed in his mind, asking God to help him learn how to forgive. One by one, the entire church family came forth and greeted him with love. Every one of them told him they loved him. He realized all of the times he had been talking to himself about how he felt, he had actually been praying.

The energy in the church made him not want to leave because he didn't get that type of love anywhere. It felt right, Mike thought as he cried out. He remembered that Jean once told him that behind every kind of painful emotion is a fear. If you address the fear, you address the problem.

For Mike, his only problem was with God, and it was time to make things right. When service was over, Lida and her grandmother took Mike home. As they arrived, Lida's heart dropped. Cali's car was parked out front. She knew it would not be good for him to be with Cali so soon after what happened at church.

"I wonder what Cali is doing here?" Mike asked, but Lida rolled her eyes and sucked her teeth.

"What's wrong with you?"

"I don't like you hanging with him. He's trouble all day."

Mike became torn and didn't want to have to choose between them. "Lida please don't do this to me right now. I'm good and you don't have anything to worry about. I will call you later."

When the car stopped, he told them both good night. Cali got out of the car and greeted him in the middle of the driveway. Lida watched them as her grandmother drove away and they were no longer in sight.

As she and her grandmother made their way home, they stopped at a traffic light. Her grandmother asked, "Are you ok, baby?"

"I don't know, I love him so much granny, and I don't want anything to happen to him."

"Don't worry about him baby, the Lord will watch over him." The light turned green and her grandmother continued, "Baby it's going to be fine."

Right then Lida screamed, "Granny watch out!"

An SUV ran the red light and hit the driver side of the car. The impact caused the car to flip as it spun across the road. It did not stop until it hit a tree. Bystanders ran over and helped pull them out the car as the SUV kept going down the road.

Seconds later, police cars sped through and it turned out that the SUV driver was being chased. One of the police cars stopped to assist and called for the ambulance. Lida and her grandmother were rushed to the hospital and her grandmother was sent to ICU.

As those events took place in Lida's life, Mike was changing clothes and getting ready to leave with Cali. As he walked out of his room something told him to leave his pistol. Not wanting to take any chances he took it anyway. Carlos was still roaming around the city and they hadn't yet settled their beef. Mike got into the car and the two rode out. It was almost midnight and Cali hadn't said too much to Mike. He then asked Cali, "Where we going man? I'm tired and I ain't trying to get into nothing tonight."

Cali patted him on his chest with the back of his hand and said, "Check this out, I told you I was going to handle that Carlos situation right?"

"Yea."

"Well, it's done."

It did not register to him what he was talking about at first. Mike then stammered, "What? Man Cali, what did you do?"

From the silence that followed, Mike knew it was bad. He knew that when Cali took things personal such as Carlos causing him grief nobody was going to have a good day. Mike repeated himself, "Cali what you do man?"

Cali wasn't ignoring him, his focus was on what he saw in his side view mirror. "What's wrong with you man?" Mike turned to him concerned about the silence. He noticed a set of headlights had appeared behind them. Quickly Cali said, "Be cool bro, whatever happens, keep your mouth shut."

"What you mean whatever happens? Cali, what you talking about?" The red, white and blue lights flashed as the siren went off. Cali pulled over and Mike became anxious. "Cali man, I got the strap on me. I'm stuck man." Mike realized then that he should have listened to his first thoughts and left the gun, now he was going to have to deal with the consequences.

Cali said while continuing looking forward he mumbled under his breath, "Give it here Mike."

"Man I can't let you do this."

"Look, I told your moms that I will watch out for you and I am. Just promise me one thing. Get the hell up out of M.C. man. I'ma take this one for you but you have to do that for me."

As much as he didn't want to do it, he knew he wouldn't be able to take being locked up. Cali knew he had warrants but his little brother had gone through so much he had to give him a chance to make it out. That night at the police station turned out to be the longest night of Mike's life. He endured hours of questioning before they released him. Cali took the charge like a "G" and never implicated Mike.

When he got home, Jean was in the kitchen crying her heart out. She looked up and saw Mike and her words were "Boy, where the hell have you been!? I've been calling all around town for you all night. Plus, Lida has been calling every hour for you." Mike didn't know what to tell her. He sat down next to her and explained what had happened. Jean went from crying and being worried to mad and disappointed. Finally Jean said, "You need to call Lida and find out what is wrong with her. She wouldn't tell me anything."

Mike ran upstairs and called her house but the line was busy. Something wasn't right. Mike began to panic. He tried calling again and Lida finally answered. When she heard Mike's voice, she started crying. "Baby where you been? I've been calling you all night. Why weren't you there when I needed you?"

Mike tried explaining, but he couldn't get a word in as he tried telling her to calm down. Lida's words cut when she said, "Don't you dare tell me to calm down. When I needed you I couldn't find you. While you were out running around with your homeboy, me and my grandmother were in a car accident."

Mike's heart dropped when he heard that. He

tried to explain even more "I'm so sorry. I can explain. Are y'all ok?"

"No I'm not ok, we are not ok! My grandmother is dead Michael, and you weren't here for me when I needed you the most! I was with you when you needed me and now that the tables were turned, you left me hanging. I hate you!"

Mike's heart broke when she said that. "Lida please listen to me!"

The phone went dead and he felt numb inside. The girl he loved screamed that she hated him, and that was more than painful. Mike never imagined that Lida would ever need him the way he needed her. He wondered why it all had to happen to him. Things were just starting to come together for him.

Mike spent the next few weeks trying to reach Lida, but she would not accept or return his calls. Every day he felt more and more alone without her, and not just that, Cali was sentenced to five years after taking a plea agreement. To make matters worse, Tiny told him Lida went back to Louisiana. He had lost everything that mattered to him. He owed Cali for what he did for him. His choices had finally caught up with him and everybody around him suffered. The anguish of not having the people he loved gave Mike the motivation to get out of Michigan City. There was nothing left for him in

Indiana. He couldn't make up for all the wrong he had done, but he was going to be somebody.

Over the next year, Mike became withdrawn from everyone. Shawn and Nika rarely talked to him. They heard rumors that Cali had something to do with Carlos coming up missing but when they asked Mike if he knew anything about it he said no. Mike swore to them that he didn't know what happened, and he didn't. Mina tried to help change their minds by telling them she believed him. She said, "A mother knows her children and if Mike said he don't know where Carlos' whereabouts, he didn't."

It hurt Mike more to have his brother and sister against him, but that only fueled his fire to be the best he could. He threw himself into graduating and going to the military. He no longer wanted to get close to anyone. He didn't want to be let down anymore.

CHAPTER 7

Twenty Years later

Mike is now known as Dr. Michael Henderson. Life changed for Michael after he graduated high school and went off to basic training for the Army. He left Michigan City and vowed never to look back. He and his wife Rachel have been married for fourteen years now. Although some might call it cliché, Mike would tell you that from the moment he met her it was love at first sight. He knew from the moment he laid eyes on her that she would be the woman he would marry. Rachel was eighteen when they met and Mike had just turned twenty, not even a week earlier. They met in an awkward moment at a gas station while Mike was stationed at Fort Riley, KS.

The moment they collided at the register at a Quik Trip their fate was sealed. Rachel was a budding Pre-Law student and Mike was a Sergeant on the fast track to advancement. Some would say they were meant for each other. Mike ended up doing five years in the Army and took the smart route and used the college money to put himself through school. He and Lida had not spoken for years and it wasn't until he started contemplating moving back to Indiana that Lida even crossed his mind. He had grown so cold after their break up that he did everything he could to keep his mind off of her.

He thought about Lida from time to time, since at one point he did think she was the one. After finishing school Mina fell sick and was diagnosed with HIV thanks to Carlos. Who would have thought that after all of the cheating he accused her of he would actually be the one to bring it home. Mike and Rachel moved back to Michigan City to help take care of Mina. It was unfortunate but it took her getting sick for Mike to finally reunite with Shawn and Nika. Mina made them promise to reconcile and after a series of heart to hearts the trio settled their differences. Shawn and Nika eventually moved out to Miami to start their own record label. Having Mike back in town gave them the chance to pursue their dreams. The twins resented Mike for leaving them behind while he went off to the military. Vying to never return to Indiana kept him disconnected from everyone. Mike also had the chance to clear things up with Lida who had also moved back. She only moved back after she heard Mike had gone off to the Army. He finally got a chance to tell her what really happened the night of the accident. She was just as hurt as he was, but they understood that their lives had to go on.

Being able to rekindle their friendship meant a lot to Mike. No one outside of Lida knew Mike as well as she did and even though they couldn't be together they agreed to remain friends. Lida always knew what he needed to hear and she always understood him. It was like time had stood still when they were together, but his allegiance was to his wife and children. Many instances he wanted to tell his wife about his past with Lida, but didn't because he wasn't sure he wanted to tell her everything. He knew he wanted Lida to always be in his life, but he was not going to do anything to disrupt his home.

To most, Mike and Rachel were the perfect example of African-American progression. After obtaining his PhD in counseling, Mike had become one of the most successful therapists in Northwest Indiana. Rachel, after finding out she was pregnant, gave up her dreams of being an attorney to become a mother.

After seven years of being a stay at home mom, Rachel decided she had put off her dreams long enough. She went back to school to become a Nurse Practitioner. She and her husband had an accomplished life. Mike was proof that anyone could make it out the hood. Rachel was just as driven.

She had the next ten years of their life planned down to the smallest detail. According to her, it would take hell and high waters to detour her from that plan. The power couple was envied by many people in the city as were their twin daughters, Alana and Allison who both went to private school.

Over the years, Mike became infatuated with fine linen. Inside their house, he and Rachel had a room dedicated to their wardrobe. Mike, with his tailored suits, silk ties and the finest of snake skinned shoes, spoiled himself as much as Rachel did herself.

One Sunday morning, Mike got up earlier than anyone else. That morning the sky was a shade of grey he had never seen. The house was silent, this was the only time of day that he could find peace and quiet. Mike made his way to the wardrobe room to get dressed. He thought to himself, 'Service better not run over today, I'm not even trying to spend all day in church.' He stood in the mirror fixing his tie and admired the work of art that was him. A conceited and overly fellow he was.

He didn't think anyone needed to look as good as he did from the clothes he wore and the way they fit him, it was all about him. Mike was aware that a lot of people did not like his personality but after enduring what he had been through, he could care less. They didn't know his struggles and he wasn't going to tell them.

Suddenly, his alarm went off and it dawned on him that he forgot to pick up Mina birthday gift. He grabbed his phone and made a note to pick it up before Tuesday. One thing Mike hated, was being late. He could not stand for things to not go as planned and he detested not being on time. That was one reason why he always got up before the rest of the family. He knew with three females in the house, the odds were somebody was going to be late. Leaving out of the dressing room, he went back to his bedroom on the main floor. Rachel was still sleeping, just as he figured. He watched his wife and thought to himself how lucky he was. He loved everything about her. Even when she was pissed off, she looked sexy when she was mad.

He went over to the bed and leaned over to kiss her on the neck. As he took in her perfume, he thought she even smells and looks sexy when she sleeps. Mike knew she was a light sleeper, but for some reason it never crossed his mind as he leaned in closer.

Just as he was about to kiss her, she jumped up and smacked him on the cheek. "Oh Michael, didn't I tell you not to sneak up on me when I'm sleeping?" She knew he was just kissing her; he had done it every morning since their honeymoon.

"I was just saying good morning beautiful." She gave him a smile and he did a James Brown impression while singing, "It's time to go to church."

Laughing she replied, "Alright, alright, I'm up."

Rachel yawned and stretched across the entire bed. Now to Mike, Rachel was easier to get up than the twins. It was as if they took sleeping pills on Saturday night so they wouldn't have to get up on Sunday morning. As he made his way to the top of the stairs he yelled out, "Girls come on, it's time to get up." He went in Alana's room and slipped the pillow from under her head as he yelled, "Get up!" She did not move, so he smacked her on the head with the pillow.

She jumped up shouting, "Daddy dang, you play too much. I'm up."

He laughed as he walked through the connecting bathroom to Allison's room. Mike did the same thing to her and she too, repeated the actions of her sister. As he headed down through the hall, he shouted, "Y'all get downstairs. It's time for breakfast and I'm not going to be late today. If you are not ready when it's time to go, you will be walking."

It was nine thirty and Mike now fully dressed was becoming irritated and impatient. Pacing back and forth, he kept looking at his watch as he tapped it. He knew it took about twenty minutes to drive to church. The sound of his ladies getting ready flooded the house. When Rachel emerged from the bathroom Mike smiled. She was just as beautiful as the first time he laid eyes on her. Coming out of his trance, he turned and yelled out to the girls, "Let's go! The train leaves in two minutes."

Rachel hated when he rushed her, but she knew he would leave them. If she knew anything about her husband, she knew he couldn't stand being late for anything. She watched him sit in the car as he normally did. She stared at him and thought about the life they had. She would have preferred not to be going to church but she wasn't going to tell him that. She grew up in a church but she saw enough hypocrites for a lifetime. She was going because of tradition, and out of submission to her man. She knew the role that was mapped out for her as a deacon's wife, it wasn't all it was cracked up to be. She felt like something was missing and Mike used to be so exciting, now everything with him was so mundane. Mike felt things were different as well. He missed his wife being at home, but after bringing up two kids, her career was her priority.

She initially went back because they needed the extra money, but now they didn't and Mike didn't see the need for her long hours. Mike didn't like her devoting so much time to work although he was a direct contradiction, spending hours on end at work himself. Rachel had plans of her own and would make them manifest whether he liked them or not. She knew it was his drive and determination that attracted him to her, and she never thought she would find herself unsatisfied.

Mike blew the horn and as soon as he put the car in reverse, they all ran outside. He put the car in park and got out and opened the door for his wife. He hoped that this wasn't an indication of how the rest of the day would be.

The church sermon was a typical one and as usual, Rachel and the girls were ready to go. Like always, Mike was in the parking lot talking to some of the other deacons. She took matters in her own hands. Rachel came up behind him and slipped the keys out of his pocket. He looked and acknowledged her and signaled to tell her one more minute. As much of a stickler he was about time, she loathed the idea of having to wait on him. Every Sunday, they waited close to an hour for him to finish talking. She became irritated as her husband still ran his mouth.

She drove up next to the curb and leaned towards the window giving him that 'I'm ready to go' look. He noticed the signs of an attitude coming and wrapped up the conversation. She got out and he jumped in the driver seat and they were on their way.

He could tell she was pissed. She had a lot of cleaning to do when they got home. No matter how clean the house was, she still cleaned it herself. She was-diagnosed and O. C. D. had everything to do with it.

Rachel whistled and tapped on her bible sitting in her lap. "What's wrong with you?" He asked.

"Nothing." She mumbled, but he knew her and as sure as hell was he, this wasn't going to be the end of it. Before they made it home, they stopped at Al's grocery store. The girls did not want to get out, so Rachel and Mike went inside.

Upon entering, women turned their heads at them. Rachel knew they weren't looking at her and Mike acted as if he didn't notice. He pushed the cart as they walked around for a few, picking up things for dinner. As Mike handed Rachel the money to pay for the groceries she thought, why is he acting like he don't see these hoes staring? As she cut her eyes at him. Mike felt her mugging him and he already knew what she was thinking. The longer they waited in line the worse it got. The way women smiled at Mike drove her crazy and it took everything in her not to pop off. Most of them were half dressed and half his age. Look at him eating it up, she thought as she glanced back at Mike, wishing he would crack a smile. He put their items on the conveyor and in a bold move the cashier spoke past Rachel to Mike, "This item does not have a price on it, sir."

"Ma', the tag said $3.99." Mike replied, flattered that she was feeling him.

"It is?"

"Yes it is."

"Since you cute and all, I will take your word

for it."

Rachel snapped on the young lady, "Heffa you got a lot of nerve, that's my husband you're talking to. If you don't wipe that smirk off your face, I'm going to reach over this counter and whoop the hell out you. You hear me?"

The cashier was stunned, she stuttered and stammered fumbling there items as she tried to hurry and check them out. Mike thought to apologize to the young lady who was obviously terrified that Rachel would keep her word. Again he could feel Rachel deadly stare beaming at the side of his head. "I wish you would say something else." Rachel grunted through her teeth. She didn't care who all heard her, in her mind she deserved it.

"I'm so sorry ma'am, I thought you were his sister or something, please forgive me." The cashier pleaded.

"Whatever, just give me my change." Mike grabbed the bags and they both exited the store. The trip home was awkward. Rachel was more upset with Mike for not checking the lady than she was for her hitting on him. He should have known better. Mike enjoyed the flattery and many women wanted him, married and single. Rachel's insecurities with Mike and other women went back to a situation that took place at church earlier that morning. She saw how he kept watching his phone during service. Why is he steady messing with that phone? Let me find out he's dumb enough to be texting one of the birds in church. Rachel was annoyed the whole service.

When they got in the house the girls went to their rooms, and Rachel went straight to the kitchen. Mike went to the bathroom. While he was away she slipped her hand in his coat pocket and checked his phone. To her disappointment he had no new messages. She knew she wasn't tripping, he had to have deleted them. Whatever he did, he was sure about to hear about it. Rachel knew how sneaky women were and she was a live wire when it came to her husband. No female was ever going to disrespect her or her family and get away with it. Even if Mike was blind to it, she wasn't. Not wanting to let another moment pass without addressing the store incident, Rachel stood by and waited for Mike to come into the kitchen and for the girls to make it all the way upstairs. She slammed cabinet doors and banged pots just to get his attention. In the middle of her tantrum, Mike walked out of the bathroom back into the kitchen. He grabbed a can of soda out of the fridge, leaned over the island countertop waiting for her to explode. She still did not say a word. Mike knowing it was going to get worse before it got any better, took matters into his own hands.

Sitting down at the dining room table, he looked over and said seriously, "Alright Rachel, are we going to talk about this? You have been acting real goofy since we left the store."

She slammed a steak knife into the sink then replied, "Stop calling me goofy!"

"I didn't call you goofy. I said you were acting goofy. There's a difference. Now, tell me what is bothering you?"

Rachel stood staring across the room and finally said, "Why did you keep messing with your phone during service, huh? You kept checking it, I swear you looked hella suspect. Who were you texting? Who is she?"

"Are you serious right now?"

She gave him a look that screamed, 'Do I look like I am playing?'

He then replied, "Is that why you've been walking around with an attitude all day?" She stood silently. Mike catching his own attitude thought she better stop doing that. Finally he said, "I wasn't texting anybody Rachel and I know you already checked my phone. I was checking my email because I am waiting on some paperwork from D. C. I told you I have that trip on Friday, or have you forgotten?"

Removing her hands off the counter and

placing them on her hips, she felt foolish as she replied in a softer tone, "Oh…Yeah ok."

"So you do recall our conversation or not?"

"I'm sorry honey, but you know how I am with that kind of stuff. I ain't stupid. I know females stay checking for you. You know I love you. I don't want to lose you."

Rachel tried her hardest to get back on his good side. It eventually worked, especially when she walked over to him and sat on his lap. She ran her fingers down his chest and used her tongue to make him forget what happened. Mike grabbed her petite waist and picked her up, spun her around and put her on the counter. "You know you're sexy as hell when you're mad right?" Mike whispered. Rachel nodded and bit her bottom lip seductively. "You have to trust me though baby. I got you." They kissed passionately before taking it into the bedroom. Rachel knew he couldn't stay mad at her because she had him wrapped around her finger.

Mike knew that his daddy and daughter day had to be earlier because he was going out of town Friday. He planned a day every week with his wife and a separate day for the girls. He tried to spend as much time as he could with them to make up for working so much. The girl's day was usually on Saturday.

The night before the trip, Mike was in his wardrobe room laying his suits out for the weekend. Rachel walked in with a worried look on her face. He knew she had something on her mind. He stopped what he was doing and asked, "What's wrong with you?"

Softly above a whisper Rachel said, "I don't want you to go. Can't you skip this one?"

He let out a deep breath "Rachel, please don't do this right now. It's hard enough for me to even be away from you."

"Mike I just don't want you to go, that's all. Cancel this one trip for me!?"

He hated it when she acted the way she did whenever he had to go out of town. To answer her, he simply replied, "I can't." Mike did not understand what the problem was. Whenever money was tight or anything unexpected came up, Rachel freaked out. "Baby we go through this every time. But God forbid, I pull this same stunt on you. If I spaz out about you being gone, then I am being selfish and inconsiderate. Please tell me what makes this time any different?"

She looked at her husband with a defeated expression and walked out without saying anything further. She was tired of him taking her for granted and she was getting to the point of not wanting to fight for his attention anymore.

Mike made frequent trips out of town without Rachel. He knew his wife stayed focus on her career, so he figured she didn't miss him that much. Some of her insecurities were due to the fact that her father used to be a coke dealer and before long he started using, and it affected the family. There were many nights the young Rachel spent wondering if her father was going to come home or if they would have to go looking for him. That was why she tried to make sure it never happened to her again. Her biggest fear was that Mike would find someone more appealing than her on one of his trips and not come back.

Mike had an early flight to Atlanta the next morning. While on the plane he wanted so bad to forget about the stunt Rachel had pulled the night before, but couldn't. Part of him wanted her to just leave because so often, she acted as if she wasn't happy. In his mind there was no use in staying married if you aren't happy with the person you are with. There was still part of the old Mike that existed and that part of him assumed he wouldn't be lonely too long. This was something that Rachel feared.

He knew he was a good dude and she had no idea the number of advances he received from women. He enjoyed the attention the women gave him, but that was it. His mother never married and he knew that having his kids raised by another man was not an option. He was not going to do that to his girls, he refused to be the cause of a divorce.

He was too familiar with being let down by his parents. From his father to his mother, he just had to do better than they did. So far as he could tell he had been. The many arguments and tantrums he endured with Rachel were starting to take a toll on him. Mike was glad that the twins at least had each other.

His life was not perfect, but he knew that God played a part in it. Mike knew that he had it all, and yet, his wife acted like she was blind. When he arrived to his destination, he tried to contact his wife. Rachel would not answer the phone. That was not like her at all. He continued to call throughout the weekend but to no availability. When Sunday arrived Mike was still calling, but no answer. Monday morning could not have come any faster for him. She would usually pick him up from the airport but he had to rent a car instead. He thought maybe she was at the office, she would have some explaining to do when he got home. When he arrived at the house everything was the way he left it, and that gave him some comfort. Maybe she was that mad at me for not staying. But ignoring my phone calls though, come on now. He thought as he settled in.

Just in case he decided to surprise her by cooking and doing the laundry. To Rachel that was four play. She always said he didn't help around the house enough. Mike thought, 'Just because I do not do as she asks, doesn't mean I don't hear her.' He went upstairs and changed clothes and prepared to start his chores.

Meanwhile unbeknownst to him, Rachel was taking this cheating stuff to a whole other level. She genuinely believed he was cheating so much that she hired a private investigator. She had that nagging suspicion and she had full intent to find out one way or another. In the midst of the accusations and distrust, Rachel found her heart searching for a new place to reside. That new place happened to be Marcus. She met him a few months prior leaving out of Horizon Bank. It was odd how they met. She left her license at the counter as she was in a rush to make a hair appointment. He happened to be behind her. Rachel could not believe the way he was dressed. 'No he did not come in here with some socks and thong flip flops on. Did he really leave the house looking like that? I can't…' She had no idea that he was in construction and that day happened to be his only day off. He had on socks with flip flops, a white tee and gym shorts. While she acted so superficial, she had no clue that he was worth 10 million dollars or at least his family was.

She had almost made it to the door when he walked up to her and touched her wrist. She jerked it away as if to remind him that his advances were not welcomed. Out loud she proclaimed, "Excuse me! I don't know you."

"Hold up. Did you lose anything?"

"If I had, I'm quite sure you couldn't find it. I don't travel your way." She said harshly.

"You sure about that?"

He said with his deep accent which was clearly southern. He waited for another smart remark but his eyes made it hard for her to think of an answer. Rachel had no idea who she was talking to. Marcus had money and plenty of it between his construction company and his family's wealth. With disgust in her voice Rachel replied, "Trust me you don't have anything I'm looking for. Excuse me." She tried pushing past him.

"Boy I tell you, some women." Marcus said highly offended by her rush to judgment.

He had to stop himself before he lost his cool. He stepped back a few feet and said, "Shawty you've got a lot of nerves looking down your nose at me and you don't know anything about me. Please don't flatter yourself." She could not believe that bum called himself trying to check her. Now her attitude really stank. Rachel was just about to pop off and make a scene when he spoke up, "Girl here take this, you left your license at the counter. I was trying to be nice and return it to you. The way you acting, I should have minded my own business and let you deal with the consequences."

He tossed the license to her as he walked off. She felt like a fool for thinking he actually was trying to get with her. She stared after him in disbelief. She followed behind him leaving out of the building. She stood on the sidewalk watching him make his way through the parking lot. She thought her suspicions of him being a bum were confirmed as he stopped next to an old beat up pickup truck. To her surprise he was parked behind the truck. She watched in anguish as he climbed into a brand new white Range Rover. He made sure he drove by her slowly to rub it in her face.

A few days later Rachel was walking out of the hair salon while texting her girlfriend. Not paying attention to where she was going as fate would have it, she ran into Marcus again. That time, she was more polite as she spoke, "Excuse me sir."

Again his eyes captivated her. They seemed to look right through her and the energy between them made the hair on her neck stand up. She could not describe the sensation she was feeling. Rachel hadn't had that feeling since she first met Mike.

"You didn't forget anything today did you? If so, let me get out your way." He joked.

Hoping to win him over she replied, "No, I didn't, but I want to apologize for my attitude. I was having a really bad day, had a lot on my mind. I was rude and inconsiderate. I am really sorry."

"Really, you're apologizing!? Please forgive my shock."

Rachel smiled and said, "Yes I am sorry." Trying to entice Marcus, she bit her bottom lip and asked. "You forgive me?"

Marcus knew he had her right where he wanted her. He was used to getting what he wanted, but he saw that she would be his greatest challenge, definitely one for the books. Running his hand through his short curly hair, he tilted the sunglasses down at her. He then asked, "You can let me treat you to lunch! I would love to get to know you, I think that will make us even." Rachel was impressed. His 6'2" fit perfectly in his black hoodie and sweat pants. His cologne was subtle and she stood close enough to take him all in.

Finding herself being enticed she replied, "I don't think my husband would appreciate that too much."

"Does he appreciate you?" She contemplated his question for a moment as she often asked herself the same thing. He sensed some hesitation and choosing not to delay her any further he left the decision up to her. He gave her a smile and handed her one of his business cards. "If you change your mind, give me a call."

Rachel walked away thinking to herself, 'what am I doing? God why did he have to be so fine?' When she got home, Mike was there waiting in the living room. She wasn't too happy to see him. She was still hot about him not canceling his trip to Atlanta. She purposely let each one of his calls go unanswered. Thinking she could teach him a lesson and show him what it would be like without her backfired. Mike didn't even bring it up. He knew she was mad but he made up his mind to do whatever he could to repair the damage. Rachel didn't speak when she walked past the TV. She headed straight for the bedroom and closed the door behind her. Mike didn't let it get to him, he was planning something to make up for it all. She would see that he was still the best thing for her.

CHAPTER 8

All week Rachel didn't want Mike touching her. It wasn't the same anymore. Mike didn't seem to notice that she wasn't interested in being intimate, most of the time he was too tired anyway. But he did notice and he knew something was off, but didn't say anything. Mike wasn't sure if it was him or something he had done that she wasn't telling.

Daddy-daughter day landed on the last day of school and the girls were gearing up to go to camp for a week. Mike was grabbing his jacket off of the chair in the bedroom as he waited for the girls to get ready. While Rachel was in the shower, her cell phone vibrated. Mike was leaving out the room when he heard it. He walked over to the dresser and looked down at the screen. He tapped it, unlocking it. Being that it was her day off he figured it was probably someone from the office. She often times had patients get in touch with her if they needed her. Mike was surprised to see that the text was from a man. Talking to himself Mike thought 'what the hell…this broad gonna make me kill her. Who is this fool? Marcus?' The text read, *Hey, baby girl.*

His mouth fell open and his heart started beating fast. He looked at the bathroom door and back to the phone. Mike repeated that action a few times more in hopes that he read it wrong or the text would disappear, but it didn't. His mind began to play tricks on him. He was overcome with the possible thought of her cheating.

Mike didn't know what to think as he sat on the bed. He had gotten better with controlling his anger over the years, so it took a lot to make him angry. But the one thing that got under his skin was a liar. What was he going to do? He could call her on it and give her the chance to clear it up. The problem was if she had something to hide odds were she would lie. For the first time in their marriage, Mike actually had reason to question her faithfulness. These few months seemed to drag on forever. He had to make a decision. At that moment the shower turned off, logic told him that it might not be what it looked like and he didn't need to jump to conclusions. Too late, he was already there.

Mike was trained to read human behavior and he was about to put what he learned to use. He was going to get to the bottom of it. He heard the shower curtain open. Quickly he deleted the text and locked her phone back. Mike needed whoever this guy was to text her again while he was there to see how she would react. Putting her phone back on the desk, he eased out the room. He waited for another message to come through. As soon as he thought she would pick up the phone he walked back in and said, "Hey babe we're getting ready to head out." She looked up at him nervously and back down at her phone. Tucking her phone under her towel she replied "Alright, see you when you get back."

"Alright, we need to talk when I get back. I forgot to tell you I have a real important business trip in L.A. in two weeks. We need to straighten some things out before then. I'll be back."

"Ok," she responded wondering what it was he wanted to talk about.

Mike knew that if she was doing something that would be enough time to trip her up. Rachel had never seen this calculated side of him. He was angry and felt played. Rachel had no clue the kind of misery he would cause her if he found out she was cheating. Sure, he had countless times to cheat but their advances were never enough to betray his family. Now, he saw that she was more than likely doing what she accused him of doing, and to him, that was a double standard. He wasn't going to let that fly.

Daddy-daughter day was wonderful in spite of him wondering what his wife was doing. He would do things or text her just to see what was going on with her. She replied with one and two word responses. When they returned from their activities the twins went and packed for camp, they would be leaving in the morning. Rachel barely acknowledged Mike's presence. Everything about her was off but

Mike did what he could to return things to normal and allow her to get comfortable. The girls were off to camp and it would be Mike and Rachel for the next week.

Rachel's routine had changed. She started getting up earlier than him and was usually out of the house before him. Mike even noticed the perfume she wore was new. He wanted to talk to her, but he didn't.

The time had come for him to leave for L.A. He acted normal towards her up until it was time to leave. Instead of flying out, Mike took a cab to his favorite hide out spot, the Marriott Hotel. It was the one place he went whenever he and Rachel were at odds, and it was his way of giving her time.

His wife watched him drive off in the cab. She sat down and cried a little staring at Marcus' number in her phone. She didn't know what to do. She used to think that Mike, the children and her job were enough, but she wasn't satisfied. She didn't want to admit it, but she felt alone in her marriage.

Mike always used the company credit card when he went to hide out, so Rachel couldn't keep tabs on him. Mike sat in his hotel room staring out of the window. He contemplated what he was doing and what he might find, by giving Rachel the rope to possibly hang herself. Deep down inside he wanted to give her a chance to come clean. So he gave her time and space to do what she wanted.

Rachel was infatuated with the idea of being with Marcus. Just by the brief encounters, she could tell that he offered so much more than Mike did. How much more, she was yet to see, but it was something she felt she had to have. When she did work up the nerve to talk to him, she discovered that he was actually pleasant company.

What was there not to like about him? He made her laugh the way she used to before marriage, bills and family kicked in. Rachel found that she would rather be with Marcus and not Mike. He actually paid attention when she spoke and the conversations were always about her. The longer their phone conversations went, the less guilty she felt.

With Marcus, it seemed that life would be much sweeter. He gave her a reason to breathe and that was something Mike didn't do anymore. She wasn't a trophy wife to Marcus, she was just plain ole Rachel. He didn't expect anything from her.

It was two days after Mike left for his trip, Rachel had made up in her mind to finally meet up with Marcus. She knew she needed the alone time and it was just like Marcus to understand her needs. Sitting in the living room reading, Rachel's cell rang. She leaned over and saw it was Marcus. Immediately a huge smile covered her face. She answered joyfully, "Hello."

"Hey baby girl. How are you?"

"I'm good and you?"

"Kind of happy."

"Kind of?"

"Yeah kind of. I've just been sitting here thinking about you and I've been smiling all morning."

"Glad I was the one to do that for you."

The phone was silent as she closed her eyes to soak in his voice. After a few seconds of silence, he asked, "What do you say we get together? Is there anything keeping you from meeting up with me?"

"No the girls are gone to camp and my husband is out of town on business."

"So we can meet up now?"

"Yes of course." She said nervously.

"I just texted you the address. You get it?"

Rachel looked at her inbox and replied, "Yes I just got it."

"Great! I can't wait to see your smile. See you

tonight."

Rachel blushed as she hung up. Rachel thought to herself, 'what am I doing? It's just dinner I deserve to have some fun. What Mike doesn't know won't hurt him.' She hopped off the bed and she got dressed to go run some last minute errands before her date in a few hours. Marcus consumed her thoughts. It was like he was everything she was missing and was now within her grasp.

When Rachel arrived at the address Marcus sent to her, she found herself in front of a steakhouse by the beach. She was early, so she sat in the parking lot playing on her phone. Suddenly her phone rang, she thought it might have been Marcus letting her know he was there.

"Hello?" She spoke. The voice of an old white man answered on the other end. It was Roy, the private investigator she had hired to follow Mike. He said he had some information to share with her. He asked her to meet him around one o'clock the next day. She agreed and hung up with him, her excitement now high. She smiled and sat back looking out the window.

Marcus had a rule when it came to women, "no emotions." He had a hatred for women that cheated. He made a point to exploit ungrateful women that left their families chasing after what they thought they were missing. Breaking down wannabe divas was a sport to him and Rachel was his latest conquest. Truthfully it hurt him. The bottom line with him was there was nothing worse than a disloyal woman.

Although, to see her staring out the window lost in thoughts made him smile. Marcus knew he was getting to her and if he played it right, she would be putty in his hands. Tonight it would be role playing. He had included all of the details in his text messages. This was the one thing he had over her husband. He liked sexual role playing. He enjoyed taunting and teasing the women he kept. When he saw that she noticed him, he got out his vehicle and gave her a nod.

Walking to the far side of the restaurant he sat and watched as she appeared in the doorway moments later. Giving her a chance to settle in, he walked over and sat at the table behind her. He held up the menu and spoke, "You look lovely as usual." She nodded to say thank you. He then said, "I've been looking forward to seeing you. I see you're wearing the hell out of that dress."

She turned around and playfully bit down on her bottom lip. Rachel reached for her phone and texted. Be careful before you bite off more than you can chew. He read the text and held up his menu again. Marcus let out a slight laugh and texted back.

129

You talk a big game, you ready to put up or shut up? Marcus got up and stood next to her chair. He leaned over and whispered in her ear "Gimme those." Rachel's eyebrows raised in confusion. "Those what?" "Whatever you have on underneath that dress." Rachel squirmed in her seat thinking. '*Did he really just ask me for my panties*? This boy trippin.'

He laughed as the waitress walked over to take their order. Neither ate much as they continued their seductive game of cat and mouse. With a few drinks in, Rachel began to lose all inhibition and as the evening winding down she decided to fulfill Marcus' original request. With a boost of confidence Rachel looked around making sure she wasn't being watched. Marcus leaned back in his seat with a satisfied look on his face. Rachel slowly hiked up her dress and slipped out of her red laced panties. She fixed her dress and leaned in towards the table, motioning with her finger for Marcus to come closer. Intrigued by the look in her eyes Marcus obliged. "Reach under the table." She said with a grin. Marcus reached underneath and retrieved the gift. He looked down and secretly investigated what was in his hand. He looked back up at Rachel and said, "Let's go."

Once Marcus paid for their meals, the role play continued. He got up and excused himself from the table. Rachel soon followed. As soon as she closed her car door, he called and told her to get behind him. She was nervous as her conscious began

130

to weigh in on her decision making. Her mind kept telling her to get out while she still could. But the Margaritas she drank were saying 'Girl, get yours, you deserve to get yours.'

Wanting to experience the best of both worlds, she pulled up to follow behind Marcus. She smiled the entire way. Marcus owned a luxury condo downtown that sat right off the coast of Lake Michigan. Rachel's jaw dropped as she saw how gorgeous his place was. The luxury of his taste impressed her greatly. Once inside, they went in the elevator and straight to his loft.

When the elevator stopped, the doors opened. As she stepped into the hallway, she felt a light breeze rush across her back. Rachel glanced over her shoulder at him, and he gave her a devilish grin.

"What's wrong baby girl?"

"Nothing."

"You good?"

Clearing her throat, she tried to figure out what just happened. Not quite sure what to think of it, she stepped out replying, "Yeah I am good."

He didn't really care how she felt. He just wanted to make sure she did not change her mind about being with him. She was having doubts, but when he looked at her the doubts went away. Once inside, Marcus closed the door behind them and Rachel turned to face him. He wasted no time. He went into the corner and grabbed a bottle of E&J off of the bar. They both had a drink but Rachel, trying to calm her nerves drank two more shots. He walked over to her, took her glass and sat it on the bar. He grabbed her by the waist spinning her around and pinned her against the wall. His eyes penetrated her soul and she wanted him inside her so bad. A million thoughts raced through her mind. Just as she was about to let go, her cell lit up on the coffee table. Marcus noticed before she did and he turned and reached for the remote for the stereo. While trying to distract her from her phone, her eyes caught a glimpse of the light. He did not count on her seeing the light flash in the medium lit room. She snapped out her drunken stupor and suddenly her lustful state became a panic.

"I need to get that."

He smiled and allowed her to break free from his embrace. Marcus had begun to feel discouraged by the interruption. He already resented all Rachel represented and he had to make her pay. He hoped that it wasn't her husband on the other end, but for her to stop and answer the phone it must have been. It also meant he had to work faster to accomplish his task.

CHAPTER 9

Mike hated the way things had changed between him and Rachel, but lately he didn't know anything anymore. Lida had been the listening ear for him off and on and with things going the way they were he needed to talk to someone that understood him. Mike was glad to still have her in his life even if they could not be together. That afternoon while Rachel was preparing to go be with Marcus, Mike was on his way to meet Lida at Applebee's.

Mike had arranged the rental car company to pick him up from the hotel. After taking care of the paperwork with the company, he started on his way to the restaurant. After about five minutes of driving he spotted something strange in his rearview mirror. There was what looked to be a black sedan following him and his street senses kicked in. It wasn't that he was afraid, he just had a thing about people following too close behind him. You never knew what people might be up to, he knew all too well the tactics of goons sticking people up by following them home. So he did what he did and made three left turns. That was his way of making sure the other driver was going their own way and not tailing him. He didn't consider it to be a chance encounter, but he needed to make sure he was right. Something was up and he wasn't going to draw attention to himself, not wanting one of Rachel's friends to notice him. He ditched the person following him and made it to Marquette Mall where Applebee's was located. You wouldn't think that a mall would be the most discreet place to go without being seen. But this mall was a ghost town. It used to be the hottest spot in the city when he was younger.

Like clockwork, Mike pulled into the parking lot and Lida's Benz was already there. He hated that she beat him there again. Getting out the car, he adjusted his tie and brushed over his waves with his hand. Upon making his way to the door, the hostess greeted him as he searched the dining area for Lida.

She always chose a seat near the window. 'What is it about this woman and sitting next to windows?' Mike thought as he continued to look for her. At that instant he saw her. Lida was facing the window as the sun touched her radiant skin. The sunlight hit her grey eyes perfectly. He got lost in one of his stares he was known for when it came to her. She turned to him and said as she got up, "Same old Mikey, always staring at somebody."

He smiled and walked over to greet her. She gave her old friend a light kiss on the cheek and smiled back. Mike took in a deep breath catching a sample of her perfume she wore as he hugged her. They separated and walked back over to the booth where she was sitting.

He sat in front of her still grinning and said, "You still got it."

"Thank you, you don't look to bad yourself. I see you cut the curls off, I still can't get used to you with short hair." They both laughed as the waiter came and brought their drinks. They spent some time catching up, when they were interrupted again by the waitress. She brought over the food and Mike stared at the plate, and then back to Lida's face. She licked her lips like he loved. It drove him crazy. "I already ordered for you. The baked chicken and pink lemonade, right?"

Rachel never remembered those things. Lida had no idea that it meant the world to him just knowing she paid that much attention to his habits. He stirred his straw in the glass as he stated, "Yes you got it."

Mike placed his napkin in his lap, just as she did. Lida said with a big sister look on her face, "Mikey how are things and don't you dare lie to me?"

"Naw I wouldn't do that. If I did things would get weird and you know lying has never been my thing with you."

Lida laughed at that as she said, "Tell me all about it. I have nothing but time for you Mikey."

Taking a deep breath he said, "Well she thinks

I'm out of town on business right now. But I modified my schedule when the girls went on summer break. I'm only in the office a couple times a week. I had to get away from her for a while. I mean, I don't know what is going on with this chick. The way she's been acting lately has me on the edge."

"What do you mean?"

"Lida, you know me and you know I know when someone is trying to run game on me. You know I can't stand liars. This broad has got to be cheating. Some goof texted her phone and I deleted it so that he'd do it again while I was there. Of course he did and since then she's been acting hella suspect. I ain't stupid. I mean, everything is off and she has no idea who she is dealing with."

"For real? Mikey that's crazy but that doesn't mean she's cheating. Females get texts from guys all the time."

"I notice everything and I'm telling you, everything about her has been off. She changed up her lingerie, her perfume, changed the password on her phone, getting up earlier and leaving even earlier. I'm telling you, it's crazy."

"What about sex? Is she still handling business?" Only Lida could get away with asking that question. She continued, "In many marriages if someone is having sex outside of the house, sex is the

136

first thing that changes."

Mike laughed inside. He couldn't believe he was actually talking about his sex life to her. Taking a drink he spoke, "No, not really and when we do, it is like she is in another place and I am trying to find out where that is. I'm at the point where I don't even want it from her."

"Wow."

"Something does not sit right with me."

Lida took a sip of her drink and pointed out, "She has to be doing something or up to something. Not to put any ideas in your head, but something is most definitely up."

"That's what I know."

"Are you doing anything to make her think you might be cheating? Have any of your behavior patterns changed that she may have noticed? Do you still show her love?"

Mike took a bite of his food and wiped his mouth to say, "I don't think I am acting any different. I do my best to show her I love her. Matter of fact, I try to have a date night with her as often as possible, just the two of us. Lately, even that has been on the backburner. I know I'm a good dude."

"Still cocky I see."

137

"Arrogant perhaps, but not cocky. You know what I come from. Y'all had money coming up, I didn't, that's why I put so much emphasis in how I carry myself. I worked hard to be where I am and I take care of mine."

Lida and Mike both finished up their food. She then asked, "Do you think she is just trying to get your attention? Most of the time, this is a cry for help. When a woman does not have the full attention of the man she loves, she's likely to act up just to get a reaction. Could this be one of those cases?" Mike frowned his face up in disagreement and replied.

"For what? That's my wife and I give her all the attention she needs. Hell I'm only one person."

"Maybe you think you do and in actuality, you don't. Sometimes men think they are doing what they need to. But you can be with somebody for a long time and not even know that the other person is unhappy. What used to work in the beginning may not work anymore."

"I don't see how that is when she never had a problem getting my attention before."

"Why did you marry her?"

Lida stumped Mike. He closed his eyes and asked himself, 'why did I marry her?'

"I think you are reading too much into it. Let her know she still has your attention." Lida said noticing his hesitation.

"I'm telling you, she has my attention. Why do y'all make stuff so difficult?"

"How about keeping your attention? Are you happy with her? Do you find yourself wanting to be somewhere else, with someone else?"

Mike got quiet. He was somewhat guilty of feeling that way. But that did not mean he did not love Rachel. He just found other women attractive, even Lida was still as beautiful as ever to him. That did not mean he wanted to leave Rachel for any of them.

Directing the attention back to Mike she asked, "Are you cheating on her Mikey? Man up if you are and stop blaming her. You know how y'all men do." Is she really asking me this question right? Mike thought. Lida could see that he was getting agitated. He was the same old Mike, but older. She took another sip of her drink, wiped her mouth and spoke frankly, "Look, as a professional, I don't have a problem giving you advice on your situation. You know I do this for a living. But as a friend, I can't give you advice on your marriage. I counsel many couples in this exact same situation. The difference is they all admit their shortcomings. Personally, having never been married, I don't know what it's like. What I do know is it's not fair to you or your wife for you to be having feelings like this. Do what you have to do Mikey and fix it."

Lida did not leave room for Mike to make excuses for his actions, she was the only one that could say these things to him and actually get through to him. She then said, "Mikey, you can't assume just because you are getting bored with your wife that it is always going to be that way. To her, it may seem like there is something in your life that means more to you than her. Once she starts feeling like that, she is going to either act out for attention or leave. But don't be mad if you ain't doing your job and she finds somebody willing to do it."

Lida finished off her drink as Mikey held back the urge to snap. He knew deep down she was right. He didn't realize that all of the time away from home on business trips had caused them to drift apart. Mike never thought that leaving Rachel alone with the girls weighed on her that much. But the more he thought about her cheating, it made what he did seem small.

He never physically cheated, but in his heart he lusted enough to have carried on several affairs. Mike sat back in his seat to say, "Lida, I don't have the energy for this anymore. I know I am not a perfect man, but God can I catch a break? I am trying to provide for her and there isn't anything I would not do for her."

"Mikey, you know good and well you played a big part in the way she is. I am not excusing her, but if you really want to work this out, you need to take the lead on this. Once her heart is gone, it is over. Personally from everything you've told me, sounds like she is almost there."

He was quiet for a moment then he said, "I just don't know anymore."

The waitress walked over, took their plates and handed him the bill. Out the corner of his eye, he noticed a glare coming from the black sedan across the street. "What the hell?"

"Mikey what's wrong?"

"You know what Lida, I think this woman has someone following me."

"What? Boy you paranoid, stop your trippin."

"Lida I am not playing. You know how I am about that kind of stuff. I saw that same car behind me earlier. I used that three turn thing I used to do to see if they were following me."

"Are you for real? You still do that?" Lida said shaking her head.

"Probably taking pictures of us or something." Lida chuckled as she finished her drink.

"I'm serious."

"Boy, y'all are too much for me. I must admit, I can't blame her. Just be careful."

"Girl you know ain't nothing changed, I stay strapped. Don't let the suit fool you. I'm legal baby and you can thank the Army for that." She laughed as Mike continued under his breath, "So this is how she wants to play it, huh? I got something for her."

Lida stood up and said, "Well Mikey, this has been interesting."

He chuckled. He was really trying to ease his anger. Politely he spoke, "Yes it has. Let me get out of here and get back to my own investigation. I need to shake this car. If I don't, I may end up needing bail money."

"Yeah right. You're no goon anymore. Wait, I thought you were laying low."

"Change of plans, I have some calls to make."

"Oh."

They walked out the restaurant and Mike walked her to her car. When they got there he said, "I really appreciate you for everything. You know that right?"

"I know. Be careful and I love you too. Call me."

They hugged. Lida got in her car and drove off as Mike just stood there. As he stood there he considered how Lida was everything Rachel was not. That thought drove him crazy because he knew where Lida stood. He didn't want to mess things up by trying taking it there with her. He was happy that they were able to talk and that by itself was enough.

Mike shook the car that was following him and returned to the hotel. He tried calling Rachel but it went straight to voicemail. so He figured he would try again later that evening. When he called later on that night the phone picked up but strangely hung right up. All he could hear was music. So he sent her a text telling her he would be coming back early because some of his meetings had to be rescheduled. He was going to get to the bottom of this if it killed him.

Rachel accidentally answered the phone and when she saw it was Mike she hurried up and hung it up. Not wanting to be denied her pleasure she turned her phone off so they wouldn't be interrupted. "You good?" Marcus asked taking his shirt off, reminding Rachel what she was there for. Rachel nodded and dropped her phone on the floor and began to help

Marcus undress. A night of drunken passionate sex awaited Rachel as she had come too far to turn back. Her heart was no longer in her marriage, her choice was made. Before she could get back into the room, her head started spinning and she felt her stomach jerk. She looked around panicking trying to spot the bathroom. When she couldn't contain it, she ran over to the kitchen sink and threw up her dinner and all of the drinks she had. Marcus intended to give her everything he had promised and more that night but couldn't. When she awoke the following morning he was nowhere to be found. She panicked trying to get her wits about her but she had a massive hang over. As she searched through the condo gathering her belongings, Marcus walked through the door with coffee and donuts.

"Hey good morning to you. I thought you might like something to help with the hangover."

Clearing her throat Rachel grinned and answered, "How'd you know my head was hurting?"

"You knocked half of my bottle of E&J so I knew you were going to be hurting." Marcus didn't realize it yet but he had broken rule #1 'No emotions.' He practically made her breakfast, he never does that. "You know I was thinking, why don't you stay here with me?"

Rachel gave him a confused look. "I mean

stay as long as you want, this doesn't have to be a one night thing." Rachel wasn't sure how to respond. She was still in shock that she had actually cheated on Mike. She was sure he had already done it but she never could prove it. She was confused and didn't want to jump the gun to tell him yes. "Oh ok, that sounds nice. But I have to get home, my daughters are coming home from camp today. But listen last night was incredible. You really showed me a good time." Marcus smiled and took a sip of his coffee. After enjoying her light breakfast, Rachel showered and made her way back home. On the way home she turned her phone on and noticed she had a text message from Mike. He was coming home today and he wanted to talk. "I don't want to do this with him right now. What am I going to do?" She said to herself.

She had called and tried to cancel her meeting with the private investigator but he told her over the phone that he had pictures to show her. She thought she'd let it go until she saw them for herself. Before she went to get the twins from the YMCA, Rachel stopped by the investigators office. She didn't have time to stay but she just had to see the pictures. Having what she considered being evidence in her possession, she headed home planning how she would drop the bomb on Mike. He arrived home about an hour after the girls came back from camp. He walked through the door prepared for whatever

Rachel had on her mind. He wasn't sure how to feel about her not answering his calls and then hanging up on him. He knew she had been up to something yesterday but couldn't put his finger on it. The girls were in their room unpacking and she was in the kitchen cooking. Trying to keep up appearances, she greeted Mike, "Hey babe, what's up?"

"Hey," was all he could muster.

Rachel looked him up and down as if to say, 'Who do you think you are?' She countered saying, "I don't get a hey, how you doing, how was your day, I miss you?"

Mike went to the living room and she followed behind him. He sat down and said, "Come here, talk to me."

She stared at him. Her reply was more like yelling. "What's wrong now Michael? What do you want to talk about now?" It never failed. Whenever he asked her to talk to him, she would get an attitude.

"What are we doing Rachel? Haven't I done everything you asked me to do? You wanted this house, I bought it. You wanted the cars, I bought them. You wanted to work, I let you. What else do you want from me?"

For the first time in years Mike had tears in his eyes. He was frustrated and angry. The whole purpose was not to argue with her, and he even tried side stepping her questions. As usual, she would not let him get away with popping off at her without making him pay for it. Since that was what he wanted, she decided to get answers too.

CHAPTER 10

Rachel did not want to talk to Mike about her. She too was fed up. She was slowly becoming numb too. She started fantasizing herself on some exotic trip with Marcus, and she was happy. She was broken from her thoughts by the sound of Mike saying, "Whenever I try to talk to you, you get upset or catch an attitude and shut down like you're doing now."

"See, here we go again. Why does there always have to be a problem. Why can't we have conversations like we used to?" Rachel rebutted.

"I don't know what is going on with this marriage." Mike replied.

Rachel stood in front of Mike with one hand on her hip and her lip poked out. "I think maybe we're just on two different paths. We never see things the same anymore. You always want to talk about something, making me feel like I'm the problem. I AM NOT THE PROBLEM!" She shouted.

"Then what is?" Mike asked.

"I don't know doctor, you seem to have all the answers. Why don't you tell me so we can be on the same page? I am tired of going back and forth about what's wrong with this marriage. I'm just tired of you!"

Mike looked up at her. He was confused, he was the one doing all he could and she didn't care. Standing to his feet, he said softly, "I am going to ask you one question. And I'm only going to ask you once, so be careful how you answer it." He paused. He wasn't sure if he could even put her and cheating in the same sentence, but he knew what he saw and needed to know.

"Well I'm waiting." She spouted.

"Are you cheating on me?"

The look of insult covered her face. Was he actually accusing her of doing what she thought he was doing? She knew all about him staying at the Marriott and she knew about the meeting at Applebee's. She had all the information she needed.

However, Mike continued to stare at her as he waited for an answer. Instead he got, "You know what Mike? Screw you! I've been dealing with your nonsense for too long. You don't deserve me and ever since I went back to work, you've been acting real extra. I can't. I just can't. I'm not going to do this anymore. You make me sick!" Rachel exploded, verbally assaulting him with all of the bottled up frustration she was holding in.

Before she could get another word out, tears gushed out from his eyes and stampeded down his cheeks. He snapped full of anger. Mike grabbed her by the throat and threw her against the wall. He pinned his forearm on her chest using his body weight to keep her there. He didn't want to hurt her, but he was going to make his point clear. As he suppressed his rage his voice spoke to her core. "First of all, don't forget who the hell you are talking to. I don't know what has gotten into you Rachel, but you better get it together before I choke it out of you. Now, we can talk about this or you can get the hell out my house." He let her go and she placed her hands under her neck. Trying to avoid the confrontation, Mike turned to her and said, "You know what? I'm going to leave right now before I kill you."

Mike left the house and Rachel ran to their bedroom. She had never seen Mike so angry before. What hurt the most was the children were standing in the doorway watching her gather clothes. She had to explain what was happening. Alana walked over to her and asked, "Mama, what's wrong? Why is daddy so mad?"

"It's ok baby. Mama just needs a hug." The girls went to her and she squeezed them tightly. She then asked, "You girls want to go to granny's?"

They nodded their heads. They were smart and they knew what was going on, but in order for their parents to work things out, they'd agree to anything. Rachel told them to go pack as she called her mom to tell her she was on her way. She didn't want to think about Mike. She was almost glad that happened because she was tired of living a lie.

Mike was pissed, he drove around the city and went down to the pier for a couple hours. The only thing he could think to do was get in touch with Lida. He felt bad about what he did to Rachel, but she had proven his suspicions by her reaction to his question. He needed to talk to Lida because she always knew how to calm him down. When he got to her place, he was still in a daze.

When she opened the door she was dressed in a long t-shirt and boy shorts. The sight of Lida in that t-shirt was already calming him down. Just being there with her made it easy for him to come to himself. The way she looked made him want her. when she welcomed him in, it did something to him but he was there for another reason. He would not dare take advantage of the opportunity to cheat, even if he and Rachel were at odds.

He had Lida's full attention. She saw his eyes were bloodshot red from crying, and that made her angry for him. She knew he was agonizing over Rachel. "Come on in and sit down Mikey." When she closed the door, he stood briefly in a daydream before she snapped him out of it. He followed her into the living room and sat on the couch. Her house was cozy and at that moment his mind flashed back to the time she invited him into her bedroom. She sat beside him and said, "Tell me what happened."

"Lida I asked her if she was cheating and do you know the only thing she could say was, 'Screw you Mike?" Lida did not say a word. She did what she always did when they were that close, she played in his hair and rubbed small circles on his back as a comfort. Mike always loved that. He was glad that she was there for him as she had been many years ago. Mike said, "I tried my best to provide for her and she doesn't appreciate it. After all her snooping and finger pointing, I find out she is the one cheating. I'm done!"

By the way he said that Lida knew he was serious. Mike gazed into her eyes and reached over and kissed Lida passionately. Her kisses were inviting and sorely needed. As much as he tried to resist Lida, he could not help it. She yearned for him too. She gave in, pushing Mike back off of her, she turned the tables straddling him and kissing him back.

Just like Mike did when he was in her room all those years ago, the kisses and teasing came to an abrupt stop. 'No please don't do this to me again,' she thought. Lida not wanting to give up, she gave him a desperate stare. He looked up at her and said, "Lida, I have always loved you and as much as I want this, I can't. This ain't how this is supposed to go

152

down. I can't put you in the middle of this. Let me handle this situation with her before we cross this line. There's nothing I want more right now than to be with you but I have to clear all of this up. Do you understand?"

"Mikey you know I love you too, you know I'll wait for you baby. Just promise me you won't disappoint me. Like I did all those years ago, I will wait for you until you get your mind cleared."

"That's my word. You have always been there for me and I got you. Just let me tie up these loose ends."

Just like she did years ago, Lida held him down. Lida understood. It didn't make it right, but she understood.

"Ok baby."

"I have to get out of here before I lose my mind." Mike lifted her shirt and rubbed his fingers down her stomach, biting his bottom lip. He stood up and Lida did too. She wrapped her arms around him and they kissed again. Mike pulled away and said, "Let me get out of here before I change my mind. I have to handle this and I promise I will make things right."

Mike drove around for the rest of the night trying to clear his head. The more he thought about

Rachel cheating, the harder he cried. It didn't feel right, but she told him all he needed to hear and that cut him like a knife. He made it home just after midnight. When he got there, he saw the house still tore up from earlier. He went in the cellar and got a bottle of Hennessey. Confused and unsure of what to do, he hoped to find a solution at the bottom of the bottle.

While Mike was drinking away his problems, his wife was back in the arms of Marcus. She had already had a few shots of Tequila before she arrived. Her emotions and hormones were all over the place. Marcus opened the door dressed in jeans and wife beater with a drink in hand. He was glad to see her. He could tell that she had been drinking and it wasn't going to take much to take her down this time.

He welcomed her in and they headed over toward the couch. He stopped and spun her around kissing her passionately. In a trance, Rachel relinquished herself to him. Tipsy, emotional and in desperate need of affection she begged him to take her. Another drink and a few minutes later, her clothes were on the floor. He paused and said, "I'm gonna take care of you don't worry."

From that point on, it was all about her and the girls. No more being a faithful wife to a man that didn't appreciate her. She deserved to be happy. She never thought of herself as selfish but that night, she was in need and Marcus aimed to please. The next morning, she awakened to breakfast in bed. Marcus sat in a nearby chair admiring her. "Good morning, beautiful." He said smiling.

Rachel's head was pounding but this time she remembered every moment from the night before. She was happy with her decision and nothing could ruin this moment for her. She was glad that it was Marcus that awakened her.

"Here is your breakfast."

"Thank you."

Rachel felt like it was all a dream and she didn't want to wake up. He got up, gave her a kiss and said, "I have a few errands to run this morning. You can stay as long as you need. The key is over on the dresser, lock up when you leave." Rachel couldn't believe it, he was already proving to be the best option. She smiled and blushed as he walked out of the door. "Ok thanks. Bye sweetie." When the door closed, reality set in. She needed to get Mike to let her go. Her morning started off great but there was still something she had to do and how that would turn out could ruin her whole day. She enjoyed her breakfast and got up and showered.

Rachel was sure Mike would be home waiting for her, perhaps with flowers and an apology. But, none of that mattered to her anymore.

She took the key off of the dresser and left for home. The closer she got to the house the more confident she was in her decision to leave him. Rachel didn't believe she belonged there anymore. Parking her car at the edge of the driveway, she sat there for a minute. How was she going to get Mike to give her a divorce? He was going to flip out about her taking the girls away. She was in for a fight. She knew he wouldn't sign any papers or move out the house. Well here goes nothing, better go get this over with, Rachel thought as she went in the house.

Mike sat on the couch still in the clothes he had on the day before. He glanced up and barely acknowledged her. She cut her eyes and scoffed, "Hmm, you still here?" He ignored her. He was so drained that he didn't have the strength to argue. She continued, "Look, I'm leaving and I don't care what you say. I've carried you long enough and I deserve better. Me and my girls are going to be better off without you."

Mike still remained silent. This broad cannot be serious, he thought. Much to her surprise, he acted like he didn't care. She taunted him with her looks of disgust.

He finally spoke, "Why you still here? You made your decision and there's nothing else to talk about right? So, get the hell out my house!"

She was stunned and he looked up at her like he wanted to snatch her head off. But she wanted to go and he had no intentions of stopping her. Rachel had succeeded in bringing him down. He was tired of trying to hold onto someone that didn't want to be held. Rachel really thought Mike would put up a fight. Part of her actually hoped he would try to change her mind but she was wrong. He was past ready for her to leave. Mike wasn't sure how much longer he could keep his cool.

Adding some volume and base to his voice Mike asked, "Why the hell you still here? Didn't I say get the hell out my house? Are you hard of hearing or just stupid?"

"When did you start talking like that?"

"Look you made your decision, we don't have anything else to talk about."

"You made my decision for me when you stopped taking care of my needs. I'm done Michael. I am so through with you and please, don't try to change my mind. You'll hear from my lawyer."

"Get out! Less talking, more walking!" Mike said slamming the remote on the table and standing to his feet.

Rachel was shocked. Mike sat back down and went back to watching TV. Seeing that she wasn't getting anywhere Rachel conceded and turned to leave. She walked slowly to the door but before she left she had to make sure he felt the same hurt she did. She went back to where he sat and proclaimed, "This is all your fault! If you would have taken care of me, I wouldn't have to look somewhere else for attention. I know you were with that hoe! You dirty as hell for that!" She didn't get anything from him. Not to be ignored any longer she got in between him and the T.V. She yelled at him, "I hate you! Do you hear me? You make me sick!" Mike leaned up and slowly placed the remote back down on the table. As much as he wanted to lay into her, he just didn't have the fight in him to do so. Rachel then said, "Unlike you, I know where my loyalty is and you did your dirt, now you have to pay for it."

He looked at her confused, "What are you talking about?"

Rachel opened her purse and dropped a blue folder on the table with a vindicated look on her face as if she'd nailed the hammer in his coffin. "What now? Who is she? I hope it was worth it."

He looked at the picture and saw that it was Lida. He laughed as he looked at her. He then replied, "That is Lida. She is my home girl from high school. She is also a relationship counselor. While you have been stressing me out with all this nonsense, I was meeting with her trying to find a reason not to leave you goofy!

Please tell me, this isn't what you were going off of? I swear Rachel, you hella stupid. I was trying to save our marriage while you were trying to get revenge. I swear to god if it weren't for my girls I would kill you right now! After everything you put me through. You need to leave now before I get beside myself."

Rachel's heart sank. She could not believe that she was wrong. It couldn't be, he had to be. She had all the evidence to prove it. It didn't matter anyway, Marcus was her choice and he was twice the man Mike was. "Whatever Mike, I know you lying. I'm not stupid, I'll see you in court."

"Rachel, you can believe what you want, but you know me. And one thing I am not, and that's a liar. But we good though, you go ahead and do you. Kill yourself! You dead to me. Now get out!" Mike had enough. He wasn't going to continue to have this conversation with her any longer. And if he stayed she would keep talking and he wasn't trying to go to jail that night.

"You know what, I'll leave. Since you say I'm never there for you, I'll live up to that and leave now. When I get back I expect you to be gone." Mike grabbed his keys and stormed out. As his car tires screeched, Rachel stood dumbfounded staring at the pictures on the table. It was over.

CHAPTER 11

It only took about a month before Rachel had the divorce papers drawn up. Mike didn't want the girls to suffer, so he agreed to joint custody and for them to split everything down the middle. He tried to make it as painless as possible for them. But, it hurt him to be without his family. He never wanted it to come to this. On the inside, he was heartbroken and torn, but he had to be strong for the girls.

While Mike adjusted to being a bachelor, Marcus convinced Rachel to move in with him. That news hurt Mike to his core, but he knew that there was no turning back. It was what it was. For Rachel, all was well with her new life with Marcus. The girls even took to him and that devastated Mike as well. He never went inside when he picked the girls up. It was too painful and he did know what he'd do if he ever met Marcus. He still spent some days trying to figure out what really went wrong in his marriage.

Six months had gone by and the girls were back in school. They were staying with Mike for the weekend so Rachel and Marcus had the house to themselves. Marcus had been acting funny for the past few days. She knew something wasn't right but he wasn't saying anything. Marcus had recently lost a couple of corporate contracts and was starting to feel the pressure. The more business problems he had, the more agitated he became. He was a ticking time bomb and Rachel didn't have a clue.

Rachel walked in the living room where he was sitting having a drink and a cigarette. She was running late from picking up the girls. She knew how Mike was about time and he hated when she was late. She walked over to the kitchen table where she thought she had left her purse. When it wasn't there she came back in the living and asked, "Baby, you seen my purse? I have to go get the girls from Mike. I don't want to hear another lecture about being late."

"Why can't he come over here and get them? Why do you have to drive all the way to the South side? He usually comes to get them why the change all of a sudden? You better not be going nowhere with Carla. You know I can't stand her." Marcus put his foot down and reminder her that he was in charge. Fixing her make up in her compact, Rachel dismissed Marcus. She knew he had probably had too much to drink. "Boy please, I'm grown." She said.

Marcus put his glass of gin down and got up. Without missing a beat, he got close to Rachel and smacked her to the floor. The side of her face was on fire and her nose bled down her top lip onto the floor. She never saw it coming and she couldn't believe he put his hands on her. He then shouted, "Woman, I will kill you if you ever get smart with me like that again. I'm not Mike, I don't play like that, you hear me?

Matter of fact, you ain't going anywhere. Sit down and act like you have some sense!"

"I can't believe you did that. You are crazy." Rachel scrambled to her feet and said, "I'm getting out of here."

She did not get far. Marcus kicked her feet from under her, and she fell face first into the wall by the door. He grunted, "Get over here. You ain't going nowhere until I tell you to. Get over here and sit down somewhere." She laid there on the floor trying to gather herself. Drunk with rage, Marcus wouldn't be disrespected. He grabbed her by her ponytail and dragged her into the bedroom. The entire time, Rachel screamed and cried. Terrified she begged him to let her go. He tossed her by the foot of the bed. She attempted to make a run for it but he knocked her back to the floor and threatened, "I wish you would try to get up."

He grabbed her by the throat and ripped her blouse off. She screamed, "Marcus what are you doing?"

Rachel begged and pleaded with Marcus like never before, but he didn't listen. After ten minutes, she hoped he had gotten tired of beating her. Who was this man towering over her? How could someone be so good in the beginning, become so evil?

Not knowing how far he would take it Rachel became quiet and grew numb as he raped her. Her thoughts grew dark as the man she believed loved her, violated her. Tears flowed from the corners of her eyes onto the bed. Marcus was in such a daze, he never noticed that she was not responsive. Rachel was too helpless to do anything about it. She eventually passed out staring at the wall.

Rachel eventually came to and could barely move but did not know how long she was unconscious. Her body was sore as the memory came back to her. She whimpered from the damage that was done. As she struggled to get up, pain shot through her body. She sat herself up on the bed, she looked around the room. Clearing her throat and turning her head, she saw Marcus. She had no idea how long he had been sitting there watching her, but there he was sitting in a chair in the corner of the room.

Still sitting Marcus took a pull from his cigarette and said, "You know I love you, right?" Rachel was appalled that he would say such a thing. She tried to nod her head but it hurt so much. Marcus then said, "You know you made me do this to you, right?"

She was glad she could not speak because she would have screamed everything that was on her mind, which might have gotten her into more trouble.

164

She didn't trust her eyes to look at him. Marcus moved closer to Rachel. She still had not moved because of the pain throughout her body. He got on the bed and propped up on his right elbow. Taking his left hand, he stroked her forehead and hair. Rachel cringed when he tried touching her. He looked at her and said, "We can still make this work, baby. You just have to stop pissing me off."

He searched her face for a response, but she knew better. He spoke on, "Don't say you're going to leave me, I can't handle that. You understand?"

Rachel began to feel guilty all over again for what she had done to Mike and she figured this was her karma. Maybe she deserved it, besides it was too late to turn back. What other choice did she have? She texted Mike asked If the girls could stay another night and she would pick them up the next day.

CHAPTER 12

The last six months were hell for Mike after the divorce, and Lida was there for him through the entire ordeal. She seemed to know exactly what to say and how to say it. She was what his life had been missing and all he had to do was keep her happy. He knew she might be insecure because of his attachment to Rachel, but Lida was all in. She was always there when he needed her. She gave him no time to miss her. Mike knew if Rachel had not of done what she had, he would have never known what they had. Mike and Lida made it official and announced their relationship to their friends and family. The girls loved Lida and she made sure that she did everything to keep them and Mike happy.

Often times, when the girls were at Mike's they would go to Lida's to hang out with her niece, Jada. Mike called Lida and asked if the girls could come over and hang with Jada while he finished up some important paper work. It was early Sunday afternoon when Alana and Allison arrived at Lida's. They were in Jada's room looking through her photo album. She wanted to show them the different places she and her dad visited. Jada turned the pages as they discussed the places.

Allison commented, "Girl you are so lucky. Y'all have been some of everywhere."

"It's not all that." Jada relented. "Unless you like having to make new friends, starting over and having to get used to a new place, then leaving on short notice. It is not all it's cracked up to be." Jada hated being a military brat. Her father Corey was in the Army and was deployed overseas, which was why she was in Indiana. The doorbell rang and Jada said, "Let me see who that is. My shoes are supposed to be coming in the mail today. I'll be right back."

Jada left the twins alone and jetted downstairs. Allison stared at a picture on one of the pages. "Ally what you staring at?" Alana asked. It was a picture of Lida, an old lady and Marcus. Just his picture alone made her turn her nose up. They could not stand him, how he had changed lately and they hated that he was partly responsible of their parents' break up. They didn't understand why their mom was with someone like him. He was nowhere near their daddy's standards and he would never be anything like him. So to them, Marcus was the enemy and when he made them call him daddy; that was too much for the girls to take.

Nevertheless, Allison whispered, "Isn't that Marcus with Lida and that old lady?"

Alana stared at the picture closely. She looked up at her sister and spoke, "Yes, that is him, but how do they know each other?"

167

"I don't know."

"She has never said anything about knowing Marcus, has she?"

Alana pondered. She tried to make sure, but spoke, "No. I can't remember her ever telling us that she knows him."

"Me either. I thought maybe it was just me."

"Should we ask Jada about it or not?"

Allison rolled her eyes, and like her daddy she pounded her fist into her other hand to say, "No Alana, don't say nothing. It might not have anything to do with her. I know we need to get out of here though."

"Well, let's take the picture and show daddy. I bet he will get to the bottom of this."

"You right."

Alana took the picture and hid it in her bra. There was no way she was letting Allison's hot headed self say anything. They turned the page in the album and waited for Jada to come back in the room. A few minutes later, Jada returned. Allison faked the excitement as Alana put the photo album away.

"Jada, let me see!" Jada put the box on the bed and opened it. "They tight!" Allison spoke as she held the shoe up.

"Look at these Alana," Alana leaned over and held the shoe just like her sister. She pretended to be impressed by them.

"Do they come in red? I need to get some of those."

"I think they do," Jada said as she was happy her friends admired her shoes.

"I got to get me some too." Allison said as she gawked at the shoes some more.

Allison handed the shoe back to Jada. Alana gave Allison the eye. She knew her sister was straight forward and if she didn't do something, Allison would let on about the picture. She held her stomach and asked, "Girl, where is your bathroom?"

"You got the runs or something?" Jada asked as she laughed.

"Naw, quit playing but for real."

"Ok, ok. It's out the door at the end of the hall on the right."

She took off running as if she could not hold it. Alana locked the door, sat on the toilet and text her dad an urgent message. 'Daddy, you done yet!? I don't want to be over here no more! Please, come get us!' She waited on her dad to text back. She knew he could be slow at texting, but she prayed not that day. As soon as she was about to give up, he texted back, 'Almost. What's wrong?' Racking her brain for an excuse, she replied, 'I don't feel good. Please, please, please, come and get us.' That was their code phrase to let Mike know if something were ever wrong.

He texted right back with, 'Ok. I'll be there soon as I finish.' She responded with 'K.' She felt somewhat at ease. She then texted Allison, 'Daddy coming to get us. I told him I wasn't feeling good,' 'K.' Allison replied.

Alana flushed the toilet and washed her hands. She went back to the room and Allison said, "You alright girl?" She and Jada laughed.

"Funny. My stomach ain't feeling right."

They all laughed some more as Jada asked, "I hope you sprayed some air freshener in there!?"

"I didn't see it."

"Ooh, I hate it for whoever goes in behind you." They laughed again. Jada asked, "At least, I hope you washed your stinking hands!?"

Alana held her hands up to inspect them. She then looked at Jada and spoke with laughter, "No, I'm going to rub them all over you."

Jada's eyes bucked as she yelled, "Ugh, no you not, either!"

Quick thinking led Jada to move her shoes just in time as Alana went at Jada in a launching motion. Allison got out the way so they could fall on the bed. Not to cause any distractions, Allison joined the fun as all the girls played on the bed laughing.

Meanwhile, Mike wrapped up the last of his paperwork. When his daughter sent him that text he knew something was up. He was glad that his work was done, but something did not sit right with him. He knew the girls liked hanging out with Jada, but that text had him wondering. He did not want to read too much into it and he didn't want to blow it off, but something was definitely off. If he knew his daughters, he knew he needed to get to them.

Mike headed straight to Lida's house. The entire drive his mind raced trying to figure out what was wrong. He thought they were going to stay longer, but he had to see his girls. When he got there, Lida answered the door. She was almost as surprised to see him at the door as he was to have to be there. He greeted her with a kiss to the cheek. She pulled away and asked, "You kind of early aren't you, what's up? Mike, this is our girl time!"

"Allison text me and said she wasn't feeling good so I'll probably just take them for the rest of the day."

"Oh ok, well I didn't know anything about that but I'll call them down."

The house was quiet and Mike knew that something must be going on because they weren't quiet at all, especially Allison. "Where are they?"

"Upstairs."

Before Lida could turn around and call out to them, the girls came running downstairs with Jada in tow.

Before they could get to their father, Lida stopped them. They almost panicked. "You girls going to come back tonight?"

Alana answered, "I don't know. Allison's not feeling too good and I don't want to leave her by herself. I'm sorry Jada."

"Aww girl it's cool. Call me later."

Lida looked at Mike confused and said "Alright y'all, I hope you feel better Allison. Mikey is there anything I can do?"

"No it's ok. I'll call you when I get them settled."

"Mikey, you want me to tag along and make sure she is ok?"

His daughters gave him the, 'Please, no,' look' and he obliged by stating, "That won't be necessary. If I need you, I will call, ok?"

Lida let the girls go and said, "Ok."

Mike gave his daughters a hug and felt Allison's forehead. It was cool and he didn't like that. It also confirmed that there was something else. All he had to do was get them alone.

"Girls let me talk to Lida alone, please."

"Ok dad. Bye Jada, see you later."

"Bye y'all, I hope you feel better."

Jada went back upstairs to leave Mike and Lida alone. Mike held Lida in his arms and said, "I love you and just looking at you right now makes me want to eat you up, but I have to tend to the girls. But, when I get back…" Mike turned on the charm and licked lips.

She looked up at Mike with a smile that said, 'Let's have a quickie.' He smiled and let her go.

"Mike, I didn't know she was not feeling well. I promise, I had no clue."

"It's ok. I know if you had known, you would have taken care of it. There is nothing you wouldn't do for them and that makes me happy to have you in my life. I mean, our lives."

"Baby, go on and keep me posted."

He kissed her and left out the house. He did not say anything to the girls as he got in the car. They didn't speak either. As he drove, he looked at Allison through the rearview mirror, noticing that she was whispering to Alana.

When they made it home, no one opened the doors. He turned around so he could see them both. Alana dropped her head and Allison stared out of the window. When they didn't speak up, he stated, "Aright, let's hear it." Mike had to get to the bottom of things and he planned to do it before they got out the car. Again, he stated with more base, "I said out with it. What was so important that made you not want to stay over with Jada? On top of that, made you lie about being sick."

Alana turned and said to Allison, "You with me on this?"

"Always."

Alana placed her hand in her bosom and brought out a picture. Mike frowned his face up wondering what she was reaching for. "Whoa! What are you doing? You itching or something?" "Naw daddy you gotta look at this." Alana hesitated before giving it to him. She and Allison locked eyes briefly as she handed it to him. "What's this?" Mike eyes scrunched up and he had a confused look on his face as he asked, "Why do you have a picture of Lida and Ms. Rosy? Where'd y'all get this?" Allison spoke up and said, "We found it at Lida's house. Jada was showing us some of her pictures and we found it while she was out of the room." "Ok so what's the point in you showing me this? Why is this so important?" Mike questioned, slightly irritated that they called him all the way to Lida's over a simple picture. Alana pointed at the man in the picture.

"What, who is that?"

"Daddy that's Marcus, mama's boyfriend." Allison said. Mike's wheels started turning as he examined the picture. Not wanting to jump to conclusions or alarm the girls, he nodded and tucked it in his shirt pocket.

"Alright well let's not jump to conclusions. I'll look into it but for now keep this between us. Ok?" They both nodded in agreement.

"Alright, let's get in here so y'all can get ready for school in the morning. Your mama asked if y'all could stay another night." They all exited the car and went into the house. Mike spent the rest of the night on and off, examining the picture. Lida had some explaining to do but he was going to play it cool and let things play out on their own. 'Why haven't I ever seen him before?' Mike thought as he saw that the picture was very old. It appeared to be taken at a time before he met Lida.

He put the picture away because he was starting to question the woman he had loved since he was young. It was odd that she never mentioned anything about knowing Marcus, but then again Mike never brought him up. If anything he only occasionally mentioned his name but nothing more. The more it weighed on his mind, the more suspicious he was of Lida and he hated feeling that way.

Mike woke up the next morning ready to begin his investigation. He had a few clients that day and it seemed that Rachel was dealing with something because she hadn't called or texted since the weekend. He was prepared for the girls to stay with him. It wasn't a big deal to him, plus Rachel was doing her own thing so it didn't concern him.

All of this new information couldn't have come at a worse time. He was feeling alone again, Rachel was gone and he was having doubts about Lida. There was no one else he could talk to. The girls were home from school and as he pulled up to the house he prepared himself to face them. He got out of the car and walked up the driveway. Before he opened the door, he knew that from that day forward, he had to put on a performance of a lifetime. He knew Lida could tell when something was up with him, so he couldn't do anything out of the norm. The girls on the other hand were a bit easier to work. He knew they would want to know what he had come up with. He was going to get to the bottom of things, and he knew he may not like the outcome. Dismissing it for the moment, he went in the house and closed the door.

Once inside he told the girls to find a movie to watch and to order something to eat for the night. They were surprised and looked at each other confused because this was out of their father's character. He gave them a smile and to them it meant everything was going to be okay. He was happy to see they were buying it and that was one thing off his list. He knew that they needed to be shielded from the adult issues because he didn't have it as a child.

He gave Alana the money for the food in case it came while he was showering. Mike walked upstairs and his phone rang. It was Lida. 'Game time,' he thought as he picked up the phone. Her voice was cool as usual as she spoke, "Hey, baby. What is my favorite man in the world doing?"

"Hey yourself. Nothing, I was getting ready to jump in the shower real quick."

"Oh ok, how is Allison doing? I was starting to worry when I hadn't heard from you."

"She's ok, baby thanks for asking. I will let her know you called to check up on her."

Lida's voice made him miss her and he wanted to see her but he didn't want to make the girls uncomfortable. "You always know how to make people feel better."

"I can make you feel better if you want me to come over." She said seductively.

'Why is she so determined to come over here,' Mike thought. Ever since he picked the girls up, she had been blowing up his phone but everything was weird. He thought quickly as he stated, "That sounds like a great idea but I think the girls are going through some daddy withdrawals, so it may not be the best thing tonight. I think they just want some alone time with me. You know how girls are." They both laughed and agreed. Trying not to be rude Mike rushed to get off the phone. "Well I'm about to go downstairs and hang with the girls. I will call you later if we don't fall asleep."

"Ok baby. Love you."

Mike paused and then spoke, "Love you too."

He hung up and went to shower. When he got out, he felt refreshed, but with new things on his agenda. Making his way downstairs, the girls had ordered two large, stuffed crust pizza, a two liter

Pepsi and a salad for him. He grinned and plopped down beside them. "Now, who is going to eat all this pizza?"

Simultaneously they proclaimed, "Me, me!"

He laughed at them as he sat between them at the table. He did not reach for the salad. He opened the box and said, "Let me get a slice." Alana looked at her sister, and they both looked at Mike. He asked, "What?"

"Daddy, you don't like pizza."

"Alana, I don't like a lot of things, but that doesn't mean I can't try them."

They all laughed as the movie was about to start. It was true there were a lot of things he had never done that needed to be done. He had taken them for granted just as he had their mother. He was so busy trying to provide the best life for them that he had not been what they really needed.

Mike had learned the hard way that time spent with family was more important than making all the money in the world. If he had realized that earlier, perhaps he and Rachel might still be together. Just the thought of her caused him to take a deep sigh.

The girls had fallen asleep on him and he was not going to move. He didn't even want to call Lida.

He just needed some alone time. He thought about Rachel. But Lida was there to fill the void she left. He was dead to the things he had gone through with Rachel, but he could not deny that part of him still cared about her. As hard as it was to let her go, he had to.

A few weeks had passed and the girls were planning their thirteenth birthday party on the eighteenth of February. The day was fast approaching and he had no contact with Rachel over the last few weeks. He left messages, sent emails, sent word through her friends, called and still nothing. He was past upset but he was also worried because this was out of character for Rachel. She usually made a big deal out of the girls' birthday, but not this time. She wasn't herself anymore and he was far too busy to be constantly checking up on her. She couldn't get with that program. It bothered him all day and as much as he tried to ignore it, he couldn't do so. Mike made up his mind to go to her.

Any apprehension he previously had, he put that aside for the sake of the girls. He knew it was risky to go see her. He didn't care how Marcus would act, but how Lida may see it. He, in no way, wanted anything to come out of him going to check on her.

The girls were at school that day and that was great. They had told him the number to the condo they lived in. He went through the lobby, which took forever. Before knocking on the door, he took the gun off safety and checked the exits just in case things went sideways. He didn't know anything about Marcus and he wasn't going to chance it. The longer he stood outside the door, the more his adrenaline pumped. Reaching up, he knocked on the door. No answer. He knocked on the door again and that time, he heard footsteps approaching. He stepped a few feet back giving himself room to react.

CHAPTER 13

When the door swung open, it was Marcus. He wore slippers, a wife beater, pajama pants and a robe without a shirt. Mike knew right then that he did not like him. His whole persona was not what Mike expected. He thought Rachel had better taste. This fool ain't even in her league. His appearance told Mike that much, but he was not there to judge. Plus he had already had plans to put someone on Marcus' trail.

Marcus gradually gave in to say, "Sup bruh, can I help you with something?"

"Sup bruh?"

"Yeah, ain't that what I said?"

Keeping his cool, Mike said, "Aye where is Rachel? She hasn't been returning my phone calls and she hasn't checked on the girls, and I need to see her."

Marcus looked at Mike from head to toe, sizing him up. Evidently this fool did not know who he was dealing with because he smirked. Mike did not blink an eye and was ready for anything Marcus wanted to do. Marcus put his cigarette to his mouth and inhaled the smoke. He blew the smoke in the air toward Mike as he said, "She ain't here, bruh."

Mike was slightly taller than Marcus, therefore, could see past him. He saw Rachel's tan Coach Bag on the couch. He focused his attention back to Marcus and placed his hands upon his hips right above his pistol. Staring his opponent in the face, he said sternly, "Fam, don't play with me. I don't care what you and her have going on, but Rachel is the mother of my kids. So, I am going to need you to call her out here, now."

Marcus stepped back, checked Mike out noticing where his hand rested. He was obviously ill equipped. He scoffed, then spoke before slamming the door in Mike's face, "Hold on, bruh!"

When Marcus slammed the door, Mike's mind searched his memory. He kept saying to himself, where have I seen him before? He was usually good with remembering faces, but he couldn't put his finger on it. As Mike waited outside, Marcus went in the bedroom where Rachel sat in a chair in the corner, staring out the window. Her will to live was stolen that day Marcus beat and raped her. She was ashamed and didn't want to see anyone outside the children.

Marcus stood in the door and said, "Ya babies' daddy is at the door. Get rid of him and hurry up."

He went back into the kitchen and poured

183

himself another drink. Rachel became hopeful that Mike came to see about her. She hadn't had a real conversation with him since their divorce. They were all two or three minute conversations. Rachel walked through the kitchen. Marcus looked at her over the rim of his glass and she looked at him with hatred in her eyes. He must have picked up on it. With a swift jerk, he grabbed her elbow and gave it a light squeeze. It pained her because her body hadn't completely healed from the last beating he gave her.

"Don't you do anything stupid, ok?"

She did not say a response as she walked off. Taking a deep breath and gathering her thoughts, she opened the door. Rachel left the door cracked because she knew Marcus would act up and there was no telling what he would do to her. Just seeing Mike made her heart yearn for him. She didn't think she would miss him that much. She wished she could leave with him and forget all she had been through with Marcus. She stared into Mike's eyes and wished she knew what he was thinking.

When he saw Rachel, he knew she was in pain. Her smile was not the same, and it touched him that she was not the Rachel he once knew. Her hair was messy and she had huge bags under her eyes. "Hey Mike, what you want?"

"Are you serious? The last time I heard from

you, you ask me to keep the girls for a few days, which I didn't mind, but that was weeks ago. Your daughters haven't heard from you and neither have I. Do you see anything wrong with this picture?"

Mike became frustrated with his ex-wife's lack of concern. He didn't realize their breakup had such a horrific effect on her. It changed his outlook of her. After seeing her, he was at a loss for words. "Mike, I'm trying to get through this the best way I can. Let me do me for once."

Mike was confused. Her mouth spoke one thing, but her body said another. The sight of her was messing with his head. He knew her so called man was listening. She might not have meant it, but her tone was undeniable telling. Her lack of communication and concern might be a cry for help, but he wasn't trying to find out. He felt sorry for her, but couldn't let that get to him. She made her decision, so it was up to her to deal with it, even if he didn't like it.

"It is not about you doing you. It is about the girls. These are your girls as well as mine." Mike asserted.

"I just need some time Mike. You can keep them until I get things together. Can you do that for me?"

"Rachel, you need to figure out what you

want to do. It's not fair to the girls or me. I don't know what's going on with you."

Rachel tilted her head toward him and snapped, "Either you want them at your house or you don't."

"It's not like that at all."

"What's it like? I am listening." She mumbled under her breath, "You never see anything."

That puzzled him and he was caught off guard when he got close enough to smell her, he could tell that she hadn't been bathing. He stood back a few feet and she gathered that he smelled her. She pulled her clothes closer to her body. He said just above a whisper, "Ooh Rachel, really? What is he doing to you to make you think you can't be a mother to your children? Are you even working right now? I know you aren't walking around like that."

Marcus made a movement, and she knew she was taking too long to get rid of Mike. Her new lover was getting fed up with her. In an unusual tone, Rachel spoke loudly, "Mike, I can't do this right now with you. Just leave and give me some time. You used to leave me alone to figure things out, so don't make this time any different."

Mike could tell that she was trying to get rid of him. It was pathetic to see her like that. He had the feeling that Marcus was probably getting angrier by the second. He didn't know what to do, but he decided to give in and he conceded that it wasn't worth it. "Rachel, you know what? I'm done with you! This is it. If you don't want to be a mother to the girls, fine! I'll give you that, but understand that's it. Don't come by, don't call, don't do anything. As far as I'm concerned you are dead to me, dead to us. You hear me? Dead!"

Rachel could not believe he said that to her. Mike's hands shook as his heart raced. He felt himself getting angrier. He gave her one last look of displeasure only to realize tears were in her eyes. He waited for her to come back, to try and change his mind. She didn't. She hoped that he would pick up on the fact that she needed him. But, she took it that he still didn't see what was going on with her. She assumed that he would never see because that was just like him. On the inside, she was broken, in a mess and hanging onto life by a thread. If only he knew that she was feeling like letting go and giving it all up.

Her hands trembled as she heard Marcus say, "Close my door."

She dropped her head and shut the door on Mike. He heard Marcus tell her to go back in the room and sit there until he came in to deal with her. It took everything in him not to go in there and give him the business. He could tell what was going on but had no actual proof and it wasn't his problem anymore.

For reasons unknown to him, he still stood there. Marcus started cursing her out because of him. Rachel did not say a word and he knew that was not like her. Mike wanted to help and he didn't get it why he wanted to. She chose that life and that man over him. Lowering his head he moved back from the door. With every step he took, he thought about all the things he went through with her. All the good and bad memories began to come to mind, he knew she was not the same person. There was no way the Rachel he knew all those years was the same one he just saw. Mike decided to take the stairs because he didn't want anyone to see him. He knelt down at the bottom of the stairs and cried.

It was seeing Rachel's condition that brought back all the things that had gone wrong in his life. He hadn't cried like that in a long time. After several minutes he noticed no one came to the stairs. He didn't know how long he had been there, but he figured it was time for the girls to be home from school.

The entire drive home he was consumed with thoughts of Rachel. Her simplicity was no more. As he pulled in the driveway, he saw Lida there. He didn't remember calling her. He really didn't want to deal with her. He had a lot on his mind and to think she was hiding something, didn't make seeing her any better. But since he still didn't have any proof he had to get himself together if he was to put on a show. He motioned for her to stay in her car because he didn't know where the conversation would lead and didn't want the girls to hear them discuss anything.

It didn't matter how Rachel was living, he was not going to talk about her in a negative way with the girls nearby. He got out his car and got in hers. He quietly closed the passenger door. He knew if the girls knew he was outside, they would come out. Since Lida was there, he needed to go ahead and talk to her. Lida spoke with concern in her voice, "Hey baby, I had to come by and see you. There is something going on with you and it has caused some distance between us. You got to let me in and talk to me. I am going crazy on this end worrying about you."

He cut her off to say, "Wait, let me go first Lida."

"Ok. What's up?"

She took a hold of Mike's hand. Mike turned his head to her and knew he had to choose his words carefully. Until he got all the information he needed, he had to watch everything.

"I went to see Rachel today at Marcus' place."

He saw how Lida's jaw dropped as did her hand off of his. When she noticed what she had done, she placed her hand back on his. He continued, "I know things between us have been slightly off lately, but she is still the mother of my children and we have history."

Those words caught Lida off guard and she interrupted him. She snatched her hand off his and popped off, "Hold up. What are you trying to say Mikey?"

Mike tried to calm her down, "Can you let me finish?"

"I'm trying to save you a break up speech because I can tell you are still in love with her and you want to get back with her."

He saw the way she bit down on her bottom lip. 'Now how in the hell am I going to fix this?' He thought. He had to regain control of the conversation. "Hold on one minute!" he commanded.

That caused Lida to stop in mid-sentence. She heard him come at her like that before, so she knew he meant business and she'd better take heed. Changing his tone, he went on to say, "Don't do that. Don't even start that Lida. You know all the crap I went through with her. I'm not trying to go back down that road again. But, I am not going to let anything happen to the people I care about either. I refuse to sit back and let those I love be…"

She cut him off and screamed out, "I knew it! I knew it! You said love. You still love her. After all she did to you, you still love her!"

Trying not to make things worse, he gently grabbed her hand and spoke to her sincerely. "Baby, calm down and let me finish." The longer he held her hands, the more he felt her tremble. He leaned in to kiss her and she accepted. He pulled back and said, "Lida, I am here with you and there is no other place I would rather be. I love you, but Rachel will always be in my life. We have children together and I am going to look out for her. I am not going to be in her life like I used to be but I'm not going to let nothing bad happen to her.

That is just how I am and you know that about me. Now, she may not be in my life, but she is still a part of my life and we can't do anything about it. We can't change what has been done, but we can change how things are done from this point on." She stopped trembling. He knew he was getting through to her. Basically, he used her own psychology field on her and she believed him. In part, he believed it too. At least, he needed to. He then said, "Today I met Marcus."

"You did?"

"Yes, and I don't like him. There is something
191

off with him."

She trembled again. The thought of losing Mike terrified her extremely. She was not going to just let him go. Lida made that promise when she came back into his life. It didn't matter if Rachel was the mother of his children or not. No woman was going to rip her from Mike's life. "What do you mean?"

"It doesn't matter, I'm going to call Cali. Cause I need to find out who this Marcus cat is."

The mention of that name sent chills down her spine. She became anxious. She never liked Cali. He had always been the one that could come between her and Mike. Even though they were older now, Cali still had the ability to influence Mike and she knew it. To Lida, Cali was the dark side of Mike and used to be the center of all Mike's troubles while coming up. It brought back memories of the many times he would choose Cali over being with her. Those memories still made her angry. She believed that Mike would still choose him over her.

Over the years, she hoped he had died or something, since he and Mike hadn't talked in so long. She knew he hadn't and she hated that he could possibly come back. She didn't even know they stayed in touch. Mike hadn't mentioned Cali's name in years, so she was under the impression that they no longer talked. Who was she kidding? People like Cali don't just leave, they live long and left a long list of hurt people.

She then heard Mike say, "I may not be in the streets anymore, but I got plugs. And if anyone can get to the bottom of this, he can."

She was going to do her best to stop things from getting out of hand. She pled with him, "Mike you don't have to do this. Why call him of all people, Cali." Lida protested.

"And why not? He has always been there for me and there isn't anything he wouldn't do for me."

"I know that, but he is trouble. He always has been. You've got too much to lose and I don't want to lose you to something stupid. I don't want you back in them streets."

"Lida, you never did like Cali."

Lida yelled out with tears, "I never liked him because you always chose him over being with me!"

"First of all, calm down. And I never chose him over you, don't do that."

"Like the night my grandmother died. You were with him and I could not find you all night. Do you remember that?"

193

Mike's head dropped, "You know I would never forget that." He said in a low voice.

"That's what I'm talking about. I'm a woman and I understand that you want to help Rachel, but she made her decision and if she needed your help, she would ask you for it. You can't be a hero all the time Mikey. She had you and she chose to let you go, not the other way around."

Being reminded of what his ex-wife did, poured salt in Mike's open wounds. That was a low blow, but he shook it off. He cleared his throat and spoke, "Baby, it's not like that. I was young and that night, like I have told you before, I didn't understand what had just happened to me at church. I needed to get away and get my head straight. As for me and Rachel, you just have to know."

There was a deafening silence. His performance was impeccable and Lida was eating it up, she would trip up eventually. The thought of Rachel in pain got to him more than he expected. Having that conversation started to mess with his head. He looked over at Lida. By the look in his eyes, she knew that he was not going to let it go. They were divorce and yet, Rachel had a hold on him that she couldn't compete with.

"You don't get how serious this is to me. I can't lose her. I just can't."

Lida took in those words and when the information was processed, tears burst from her eyes. Mike wiped her tears as she cried, "Mikey, listen to what you just told me. You said you can't lose her."

"I know what I said but listen…"

She interrupted saying, "You still in love with her?"

"Lida?"

"Mikey, I waited for you. Before you came to me on your terms, you asked me to give you time to tie up your loose ends. I waited for you because I love you with every part of me. I did all that for you and to hear you say you can't lose her makes me question where I fit in your life?"

"Lida, you have never known me to be a liar. I would be lying if I said I didn't still love her because I do, but I am not in love with her. I am in love with you. Rachel will always have a place in my heart and that's not going to change. I don't mean to sound harsh, but it is the truth. I don't want anything to happen to her. It will hurt my girls and if you hurt my girls, that's a whole other problem. I'm going to get to the bottom of this. So before it comes to anything like that, I'm trying to stop it. I have to do this." Lida saw the determination on his face and at that point, she knew she'd lost him.

"Mikey I love you and please believe that. You and the girls are all I care about and if you feel this strong about it, I know I can't change your mind, just please don't do anything stupid. I already lost you once, I don't intend to lose you again."

"I'm where I want to be and that's with you. Just trust me baby. Be cool, we together and nothing is going to change that."

The thought of becoming his wife one day was the end goal and she needed to be declared the winner. "Baby just be careful and leave Cali out of it."

"I'm good baby, I'll call you."

"Ok Mikey." She said not believing a word he said.

That was all he needed to hear from her, but he was going to reach out to Cali whether she liked it or not. "We good?" he asked.

Lida, wiping off her face, spoke with a small laugh. "Yeah baby, we good."

Mike caressed the side of her face and stated, "Please don't cry. It's going to be alright."

"I know, but right now I can't help but think I am losing you."

"No. Baby, no. Just go get some rest and don't worry, you are not losing me. Deceit and lies tore up my marriage. That is not going to happen to us."

"You right."

"I promise I will get to the bottom of this so all your insecurities can go away. Now, let me get in this house before the girls start worrying."

He leaned over and she kissed him. When he got out of the car, she waited for him to get in the house. She cranked her car up and spoke to her navigation system, "Call Dooney."

It spoke back, "Calling Dooney."

As the computer dialed the number, she waited for him to answer. A man answered, "What's up?"

"Meet me at my house right now!"

"Shawty who is you yelling at?"

"Just meet me there, now!"

"Alright give me a little bit, I'm in the middle of something."

"No put that on hold and we need to meet now. Is that understood?" Lida said with panic in her voice.

"Yeah, yeah."

"End call." She said to the phone system.

The computer did as she asked. She raced to her house. 'I can't believe this. Oh my God why? No! No. This can't be happening.' She thought to herself. When she pulled up, she parked in her garage and a white Range Rover sat parked in front of her house. She got out of her car, went over to the passenger side of the truck and opened the door. A cloud of weed smoke hit her as she climbed in. He looked at her and said, "Get in, you letting my smoke out. This purp ain't cheap."

She got in and the first thing she said was, "Forget all that, I need to talk to you?"

As he passed it her way trying to be funny, he said, "Here take this and calm down."

She looked at his blunt, and frowned as he retorted, "Why not?"

"Give it here." Her hands were shaking as she tried to get her thoughts together.

Lida took a drag of the blunt and closed her eyes and took a deep breath. It had been a long time since she smoked and it eased her mind. Taking another puff, she inhaled it longer so that the high would kick in. She opened her eyes and released the smoke toward him. Her looks told him that he must have done something wrong. For the life of him, he never understood why whenever his cousin called on him to help her out, he always did. She always had a special place in his heart because she saved his life once, and for that, he would do whatever she asked. She passed the blunt back to him and he asked, "What was so important that I needed to stop what I was doing? You act like I have to stop every time you call me. I do have business to take care of."

She hit his arm and yelled, "Dooney, what did you do? All I told you was to keep her out the picture. You wasn't supposed to fall for her. Now you got her living with you?"

"I'm sorry cuz, I couldn't help it. I know what you said but shawty is bad and I couldn't let that go." Dooney took another pull from the blunt and exhaled the smoke.

"I don't care about that. Your only job was to keep her away from him, not make him more worried about her."

"You must not be taking care of business cuz, if he flipping out over her."

Lida yelled at him, "I am doing my part! But, I can't do yours too."

"What you mean? Girl, you better sit down

somewhere. I can't help it if she fell for me. I kind of like having the broad around." Lida got angry as she snatched the blunt from him and took another pull. Dooney then said, "You need to give him some of this." He let out a harsh cough and a laugh.

"Dooney stop playing. You need to fix this." She handed the blunt back to him. "I don't want this to get ugly. I worked too hard for this to fall apart right now. I practically built this man from nothing and I will not be outdone by anybody." She said banging on the dashboard.

"I know what you are saying, but do you hear yourself? This is way past ugly and it's probably going to get worse, know what I am saying?" Lida closed her eyes to meditate on what he told her. She began to truly weigh her options. She wanted Rachel out of her and Mike's life, but she did not want to push her back into his arms. She thought more and more on what to do, and then Dooney spoke, "Wake up and talk to me." Lida snapped out of it. Dooney then said, "Well, what you want to do? I told you I have other stuff to do and I can't get it done sitting here with you."

"Alright, alright. Dooney get rid of her. Don't kill her, I'm not going to make her an idol for him. I can't compete with that. Get her to leave on her own. Whatever you have to do, just make her disappear. I will keep my eyes on Mike. Just make it clean."

Dooney took a long, hard look at her. He could not understand why she wanted Mike so bad. She was far from ugly, had plenty of money and was doing good for herself. From what he saw, that dude Mike wasn't even in her league and she was trying to fit in his life. He decided on a plan. "Alright. I got you, but this is going to cost you."

"What you mean it's going to cost me? I already gave you twenty thousand."

"Naw cuz, this is going to take more planning and I'm taking all the risk. I need another twenty."

"Twenty what?"

Dooney gave Lida a dumb look and she bucked her eyes at him. He came out and said, "Twenty-thousand. Get me twenty-thousand so I can go handle that."

Lida twisted her neck toward him as she leaned her body toward the passenger door. Her mouth was at an all-time low when she squealed out, "Twenty-thousand dollars! You can't be serious. You have to be joking." She said shaking her head.

Her outburst did not faze him one bit. He calmly spoke, "Look, like I said I'm the one taking all the risks. Business is business and I know you family but... You have to keep the two separated, and now this is business. Don't get me wrong, I love you, but I love how I live too. You are the one that wanted to take this route, not me, and because of that, it is what it is."

She hated it when he was right. He was the one that would catch the heat and if anything went wrong, he was the one that would take all the blame, not her. She let the air out of her lungs and looked out the window to think. "Hurry up. I told you I have business to take care of and you holding me up."

She faced Dooney and said, "Fine."

"Fine what?"

"Fine Marcus! I will get your money. Just give me a couple of days. Until then, don't do nothing stupid."

"Lida, I got mine. You handle yours."

"Thanks."

"I got you Lida. Just look out for me."

They hugged and Lida got out the truck. Dooney drove off and she watched him leave. She went back to her car and sprayed perfume on her to cover the scent. She thought about Mike and what he was about to do and hoped everything would go as planned.

CHAPTER 14

The days came and went following the incident between Marcus and Mike. Lida tried stepping up her game, but she was not fooling Mike. He would have been taken in by all her sweetness if his daughters had not have shown him that picture.

While he tried to get word to Cali that he needed to see him, he devoted his time to making things right for the girls and being a great father for them. He knew he couldn't take Rachel's place, but he did what he could so they wouldn't feel abandoned by her. When he wasn't thinking about Lida or being with her and his children, Rachel and Marcus consumed his every thought. He could not talk to Lida about it anymore because he feared that she could be the enemy. It grieved him immensely that he was with a woman he couldn't talk to about everything. Above that, she had a personal interest in his life, so her advice would not be unbiased. Many times, he wished he could just let it go but he couldn't.

His cell rang, and when he looked at the number, he saw the number was restricted. "Hello."

"Lil bro what's good? Man, it's good to hear your voice. I heard you was trying to reach me."

Mike's face lit up. It was Cali. "Man, it's great

to hear yours too."

"I had to use one of my private numbers because I had to make sure it was you. You know how it be."

"Yeah, I changed numbers and deleted all my contacts too. Haven't really spoken to a lot of people since I moved back."

"Oh ok."

"I know you don't really be on the west side like that no more. Let's meet up at Applebee's for lunch and catch up."

"You buying?" Cali joked.

"Yeah I got you bruh." They laughed as Mike added, "You coming?"

"Since you buying, I'm coming." They laughed and got off the phone.

The girls were at Rachel's mother's house and he was finished for the day. Mike got in his car and headed to the mall early. He didn't know what Cali would be driving and he just didn't want to be late. Mike took a corner seat near the window. He found himself staring out of the window thinking about Rachel. Once that thought came, the windows of the family centered diner began to vibrate. He looked to see where it was coming from. Making that sound was a black Harley Davidson pick up. 'Now that's got to be Cali.' Mike thought. Jumping out the truck was his friend Cali. Mike had a huge grin on his face.

His best friend came through for him. Cali had put on some muscles and was sporting a long beard like he was from Philly. The years had been kind to him. Cali walked in and spotted Mike. He stood up and Cali walked over to him with a smile. They hugged as they shook each other's hand. Cali spoke while laughing, "Ha-ha lil' brother. How you been?"

Mike sat down and so did Cali. "My A-1 since day one. It has been a long time, I'm good man."

Cali waved his hand for the waitress to come over. She did and he said, "Hey, ma."

"Yes sir, what can I get for you?"

"Can I get some lemonade and a couple of lemon slices?"

"Pink, regular or strawberry lemonade?"

"Let me get strawberry."

She glanced at him and he winked. He couldn't help but flirt with every beautiful woman he met. The waitress turned toward Mike and asked, "What can I get for you sir?"

"Let me get the same thing."

"That's two strawberry lemonades and four slices of lemon?" They both nodded their heads. She said, "Coming right up."

She walked away. Mike then said, "I see you still love the ladies."

"No doubt. Got to love the ladies."

"Only time has changed."

"Only time."

Mike was about to get down to business, but the waitress walked over, and placed their drinks in front of them. She then asked, "Excuse me, is there anything else you need?"

Cali said, "Yeah you, but not right now."

She blushed then said to Mike, "Enjoy your drinks."

Mike then said, "You know Rachel and I divorced?"

"Yeah I heard."

"I have my girls because she didn't want to be their anymore."

Cali took a drink and said, "You sure we

talking about the same Rachel I heard about you marrying?"

"Same thing I said. She used to go crazy when she felt that I was too hard on the girls. I think it has something to do with this goof she shacking up with."

Cali's eyes got big, "She shacking, too?"

"Yeah man, moved out of my bed and into his."

"Wow Mike, she didn't waste no time, did she?" Cali said shaking his head.

"It got to the point that she ignored me and the girls. I went by their place and she came to the door looking a mess bruh. It was crazy." Cali's phone vibrated and he looked down and chuckled. "My bad man, this chick I met in Gary just texted me. Go ahead."

"Cali, I mean she was actually funky and the Rachel I know has never even liked to sweat."

"That's crazy man. So who is this dude she's kicking it with?"

"The guy she is with name is Marcus."

"Marcus who?"

"Don't know. The girls don't know his last name and neither do I."

Cali was quiet for a few minutes. He took a sip of his drink and asked, "Well what do you need me to do?"

"Man, I don't know. I guess I need to find out who the hell this dude is and how he's connected to Lida."

"What Lida?"

"Lida."

"Oh Lida. Ole girl you had it bad for when you was younger?"

Mike laughed and said, "Yeah, that Lida."

"You think she knows this cat Marcus?"

"I do, but she hasn't ever mentioned that she knows him or anything. Here."

Mike handed him the picture his girls gave him. Cali stared at the picture and replied, "He looks real familiar. I think I've seen him before. I just can't place it."

"Same thing I said."

"I don't know from where lil' bro, but I know this cat."

Mike said, "Let me know what you find out. Keep tabs on him for me Cali."

Cali laughed as he said, "You know me. I got you."

Mike laughed and said, "I know you, that is why I said keep tabs."

"I will call you in a day, two at the latest."

"Ok."

"It was really great seeing you again."

"Lil' bro, you know me, always got something to do."

"I know."

Mike put the money on the table for the drinks. Cali stood up and they shook hands again. Mike left. He was kind of nervous because the last time he told Cali about a problem, it disappeared and he lost his brother and sister behind it. He got in his car and left as he thought about his ex-wife.

Rachel woke up with the determination to pull her life back together. She was finally back to work and even had contracts through a doctor's office for new patients. All she could do was think about Mike and the girls. How she missed them. Her eyes became teary eyed again, but she thought that she had done enough crying.

Marcus had been wonderful to her in the

beginning and for some reason, was being nice again, but the damage was done. She cared for him, but not enough to stay with him. He said things would get better between them, but she didn't trust him. He wanted her to go to Mexico with him and she laughed at that. No way was she going out of the country with a man that had beaten and changed her entire outlook on life. He said he wanted her to go away with him so they could work things out. God worked in mysterious ways, because she got the idea of leaving everything and everybody before he brought it up. To her, she was the common denominator in everything that had gone wrong in her life. She had to remove herself from the situation. Things would be better once she got away from Marcus. Mike and the girls could be happier if she were gone.

Oddly, Marcus never came right out and said he didn't want her to see her girls, but when she mentioned it he would frown up. Rachel vowed if she could get her family back, she would spend the rest of her life making up for the hurt she caused them. Rachel only wanted what was best for the girls and being with Mike was that, for he represented stability and love. In time, she would ask for their forgiveness with hope they all still loved her.

Just thinking about her situation brought to mind all of the promises she made to Mike, her girls and to herself. Mike always told her not to make promises she couldn't keep. She didn't get what he meant until now, he would say passion always outweighed promises. It had turned out to be true in the end.

This would be the beginning of finding the woman she really was. It would all work out and there was no other way to do it. She would not only be able to escape Marcus, but she could get back everything she lost.

Coming back off break, she saw more patients as she continued to be engrossed in thoughts. Where would she go? What if it didn't work? What would she do if Marcus figures it out? Those questions kept at her. The day began to wear down and still, she had no solution. She was coming off her last ten minute break before seeing her last patient. Silently she thought, 'Lord, can you get me away from this man and help me get my life back?'

Having said that she walked in to see her patient. She got the chart and saw the person was there because of an allergic reaction. The patient eating Brazilian Nuts almost killed them and was coming for a follow up checkup. Rachel didn't remember all she had said but at the end of the day it dawned on her what she needed to do. All she could think about was leaving and running away. She sat in her car and cried, what she was about to do, she should have been done months ago. There in her car she plotted her escape. She went over every detail.

She wondered how she would finance her getaway without Marcus tracking her. Then it came to her, Mike had given her a card for emergencies.

Rachel pulled out the Visa card and called to check the balance. She smiled and was elated to know that Mike hadn't cancelled the card. She called Marcus and he didn't answer. She figured he was in meetings. This was her chance, there was no better time than now. Calling the airport, she booked a flight to Brazil and as luck would have it, there were two openings. One was for four in the morning and the other was for two in the afternoon.

She took the earliest one and raced to the condo to hurry and pack before Marcus came home. Making her way to the front doors, she handed the valet her keys and walked down the hallway. With each step she took she prayed, hoping she would finally be free. Nothing was going to stop her and if he was there, she would make arrangements for the next flight.

Still she had to mask her excitement. She didn't need to let in on that an escape was brewing in case he was there. She made it to the door of their place and an eerie feeling overcame her, the hair on the back of her neck stood up. A sensation swept over her and she couldn't explain it. Filled with anxiety she fumbled to find her keys. Taking a breath to calm herself she placed the key in the door and opened it.

Putting her keys and purse on the stand by the door, she turned the lights on. Rachel couldn't believe what she saw.

The smell of marijuana and bleach filled her nose. On the floor she saw papers and trash in the mist of overthrown furniture. The place looked like a tornado had hit. Her mouth dropped. She kept it covered with part of her jacket so she didn't breathe in the fumes. Along with her heart beating at a record high, her adrenaline started pumping as she walked deeper into the living room. As she got closer to the kitchen, she saw a half empty bottle of vodka and a blunt still burning in an ashtray on the table where Marcus usually sat.

Panic started to set in as she called out, "Marcus honey, you in here?"

No sound was heard as her mind continued to race. She looked back at the table, then turned her head to the left. There on the wall as high as the ceilings, were splatters of blood, which ran down the wall. Her eyes became big as thoughts of Marcus being hurt entered her mind. Slowly walking further in, she eased closer to his chair and there in the middle of it was a semi-circle puddle of blood. Backing up from the area, she moaned and shook her head. Oh my God what happened?

Not watching where she was going, she

stumbled over the ottoman in the living room. Rachel hit her head as she fell on her back. She groaned softly. She tried to stand up, but she was dazed. Getting up again, she heard voices and instantly thought that someone might have come back.

She held in a scream as tears of fear overtook her. Her mind told her that she would be blamed if he was not found. She also thought that this meant she really needed to run away and never come back. She was right, she had to leave now. She moved her body backwards to the door. Once back on her feet, she snatched her Coach bag and keys. She closed the door softly and sneaked past the people at the other end of the hallway. She kept her head down as she made her way to the lobby. The bell hop spoke, "Nice evening, Ms. Rachel."

She mumbled, "Yes thank you." He looked at her, but she kept going. The valet brought her car and she sat there confused. She then hopped on the highway and headed to Chicago O'Hare airport, no luggage, just her ticket and passport.

Meanwhile, Cali called Mike at home and said, "Lil' bro, what's good dirty?"

Mike knew that was the signal for a job. Mike then asked, "Nothing on my end. What you know good?"

"Meet me at the spot in twenty minutes. I

have something for you."

"Ok."

Mike hung up and immediately had a bad feeling about it. The spot was a run-down warehouse on the outskirts of town. Mike hated it back then and still hated going there. Mike thought, 'I should not have gotten Cali involved. I told him not to do nothing.'

He went into the wardrobe room and threw on some jeans and a hoodie. This wasn't going to be a suit and tie situation. Checking his pistol, he tucked it in holster and adjusted his hoodie. He knew anything dealing with Cali called for him to be strapped. You never knew with him. He went to his car and headed towards the warehouse. His mind made him wonder what he was walking into. Cali never gave details over the phone. One thing was for sure, he knew if it was Cali, it was bad.

Mike turned off the headlights and crept down the alley leading to the warehouse. He came upon three vehicles, two black Navigators on the each side of Cali's Harley Davidson truck. Mike said under his breath, "Here we go."

He positioned himself and parked giving himself an escape route in case things went south. Checking around before going in, he didn't notice anything out of the ordinary. Silently, Mike closed the door and walked toward the entry of the warehouse. Turning the handle, he slowly stepped inside the partially lit building. He saw a dim light in the office part of the building and went toward it. He was nervous and his stomach started doing flips as he walked to the door. When he entered, he saw Cali standing with a black and mild in his mouth. He faced Mike as he stood in the doorway, "About time you joined the party, lil' bro." Cali said taking a pull from the cigar.

"What's going on, man?"

"I have a surprise for you!"

Cali stepped out the way and Mike saw a small, wooden like table with a drop light hanging over it. That was not what got his attention. It was past the table in a dark corner. There stood two of Cali's goons, men he had never seen before. Each was dressed in black and beside those two were two more men with heavy artillery on their shoulders. The sight of them gave Mike confirmation that this was bad. In between Cali's men was a person tied to a chair, with a bag on his head. Mike turned his attention back to Cali and inquired, "Cali what is this?"

"Calm down, lil' bro."

"Cali, I told you to watch him, not kidnap him."

216

With his usual smile, Cali replied, "Lil' bro, you know me."

"Yeah I do, that is why I said to just watch him and that's it."

"You know how I do it though."

"Yeah, I see how you do. Is he dead?"

"Lil' bro, you won't think how he is once you hear what I have to tell you!"

Mike assumed the worse. He started pacing back and forth, biting his fingernails. His mind told him that maybe he was going to say that Marcus used to mess with Lida or something. When that didn't fit, his mind told him that Marcus was into something crazy and had pulled Rachel into it, and that was why Rachel acted the way she did. That didn't fit either. At the end of his thoughts, Cali snapped his fingers like the gangsters did in movies.

He spoke like a true boss, "Bring him over here." His unarmed goons grabbed Marcus by his arms and toted him over to the table. The men continued to stand on each side as Cali spoke, "Take that bag off." The smaller of the two snatched off the bag. On top of his head were heavily indented gashes. Dried blood and fresh blood were in the cuts. His eyes were partially swollen, but sunken no doubt. You would have thought he had a mouth full of cotton from the way his cheeks looked. His lips were parched and cut. From where he stood, Mike could see the torture he must have suffered from the hands of those men.

Cali said, "Sucka, tell my lil' bro who you are?" Marcus held his head up some and didn't say a word. The taller of the two men took out a bat and hit him on his bruised arm. Marcus screamed in anguish, but didn't say a word. Cali then said, "So you want to be hard, huh? Hit him again." His goon hit Marcus on the same side in the same place. Mike felt his pain from where he stood. He wacked continuously on Marcus' arm. Mike didn't think Marcus deserved the pain they gave him, but he wasn't running the show. Cali said, "Let's make sure he don't walk again."

The smallest of the two took out a knife almost like a machete, but smaller. The first hit on Marcus leg sprung blood all across the room. His body shook from the pain the man gave him. Mike turned to Cali and said, "You trying to kill him?"

"No, but you might."

"What you mean?"

"First of all, remember I told you that cat looked familiar?"

"Yeah."

"Lil' bro, you know him too."

"No I don't. I have racked my brain trying to see if I knew him and for what it's worth, I couldn't come up with nothing."

"Look closely at him."

"Uh Cali, it's kind of hard to recognize him." Mike said pointing at the damage to his head.

"Think back when you went to his place."

Mike thought about the time he went to see Rachel and he talked to Marcus for a few minutes. He closed his eyes and then said, "No, I don't know him."

"Ok, picture him skinnier with dreads and a beard."

Mike closed his eyes again, and when he opened them, Cali spoke with excitement. "Lil' bro, it's Dooney. Lida's cousin, the young boy from New Orleans." Mike raked his hands through his hair as he looked at Marcus. His thoughts were everywhere. Cali held off telling Mike who Marcus was because he had something else in mind. Cali plainly stated, "Lil' bro, that's not all."

"You mean there is more?"

"Lil' bro, I wouldn't bring you here for

nothing."

Just like that, the bad feeling was confirmed. The goons moved out the way as Cali flipped the table, causing it to land on its side. His goons laughed, but Mike didn't. He tried to prepare himself for the reason, but Cali's taunting voice spoke to Marcus, "Sucka. You want to tell my lil' bro what the business is?" Marcus did not speak, and Cali hit him in his bruised face and laughed. Cali then said, "Come on, fool. You bad enough to do the deed, be bad enough to tell it."

Marcus didn't say a word and Cali hit him a few more times in the face, making spit and blood spew from his mouth. Mike never liked Cali's methods and didn't like Marcus, but he didn't want this to continue. Interrupting Cali from his torture session, he asked, "Cali, he's not going to talk. He probably can't talk. So, you tell me so I can get out of here."

Cali gave Marcus one last hit and his head dangled. Cali spit on him and walked toward Mike. One of his goons handed him a towel to wipe off his knuckles. "I always told you that I couldn't stand Lida. I told you back then that she was bad news, now lil' bro."

"What does Lida have to do with this? That's the whole reason for all of this."

Cali spoke with pure hate, "She has everything to do with it. In fact, she is the reason we kicking this sucker's ass."

When he said that, he ran over and kicked Marcus in the chest. He and his goons laughed heartily. "Pick that sucka up." The goons obeyed as Cali turned to Mike to say, "Lil' bro, she paid her cousin to come between you and your wife. When y'all were having problems, she put him on Rachel. To me, man, y'all both got played."

He stared at his most trusted friend in hopes he was wrong. Mike's life flashed before his eyes. He had not prepared himself to hear this kind of news. Feelings of hate, bitterness and resentment possessed him like never before. He pushed Cali out the way and went toward Marcus. Cali laughed as Mike snatched Marcus by the collar.

Taking out his gun, he pistol whipped Marcus in the face. Soon he realized what he was doing, he came to an abrupt halt. With tears in his eyes, he looked Marcus in the face and yelled, "I hope you live a long and miserable life for what you have did to me and my family!"

Mike released Marcus and he fell onto the floor. He was making his way to the door when Cali asked, "What you want me to do with him?"

Mike stopped but did not turn around, for fear

that the desire to kill Marcus would overtake him and he would do it. He continued to face the door entrance and with his head down he said, "Do whatever you want to do with him. I don't care."

He walked off with vengeance on his mind for Lida.

CHAPTER 15

Mike cried with anger when he got back to his car. He hit the steering wheel repeatedly as tears escaped his eyes. He could not believe that Lida could be behind something so gruesome just to break up his family. Mike lingered a few more minutes to get himself together before heading to Lida's.

He knew that love could hurt but he never expected for her passion to outweigh the promises she made to him. For the second time in his life, Lida had turned on him, but it hurt more this time. The first time, he was young and naïve, but this time he was grown and experienced. He sought her advice in help to save his marriage because she was a friend. A friend that he didn't expect to ever turn on him.

He drove around for hours and the more he drove, the more difficult he found it to drive. He could not believe it no matter how he looked at it. Lida was involved, she had everything to do with his broken family and she had practically destroyed his life. He dried his eyes and looked at his cell. It was late and he knew that at this time of night, she was probably in the living room lying on the couch. Mike got out the car and carefully closed the door. Nothing mattered anymore. When he made it to the door, he didn't knock. Mike busted through the door and Lida screamed. She let out a sigh of relief because it was

Mike. She took a closer look and noticed that he had been crying.

He spoke like a mad man, "Get up! Get up now, you liar."

She continued to sit at the corner of the couch confused. She did not understand him. When she did not move, he snatched her by her t-shirt and it ripped exposing her breasts. The sight of her no longer excited him. He overlooked her body and pulled her from the couch and held her by her throat against the wall.

"Mikey, please stop! What's wrong with you? I can't breathe."

"You don't deserve to breathe the same air I do, you snake, you liar, I should kill you."

"Baby, please, let me go so we can talk about this."

Mike was furious with tears flowing again and he could barely contain his hurt. He let her go and she gasped to breathe. Mike stepped back and slid down the wall to the ground. She swallowed and placed her hands under her throat.

"Mikey, what is the matter with you?"

"You! You are what's the matter with me. I loved you and I gave up everything for you. I have loved you since I was seventeen. Don't you know there was nothing I would have done for you? I came to you as a friend because I needed advice and I thought you had my best interest at heart, but you didn't. I trusted you when it was almost impossible for me to trust women, and you know everything I've been through. But that did not stop you from hurting me."

Lida also had tears in her eyes as she asked, "What did I do? What did I do? Huh? All I did was show you love. I was there for you when Rachel wasn't."

"Rachel, couldn't be there for me, could she? You made sure of that, by bringing in your cousin to do your dirty work." Mike began pacing the floor shaking his head. He couldn't stand to look at her and the pain he felt made him want to kill her right then and there. "Lida you disgust me, get up right now."

Lida stood up, trying to play dumb she asked, "What are you talking about? What cousin?"

Mike wasn't going to let her insult his intelligence. He asked "Who is Marcus to you?" When he said that, her face went blank. She confirmed what Cali told him by her expression. More tears flowed down Mike's cheek as he looked at her.

"I believed you with all my heart and I loved

you, but you lied to me."

"Baby, I didn't lie to you. It was all his idea. It was all him."

"Shut up! Don't you dare tell me you didn't know Rachel was seeing your cousin, Dooney? Don't tell me you didn't know anything about it when you were the one paying him to seduce Rachel."

Lida could only say, "Baby, let me explain."

She walked toward Mike to touch him and he said, "I hate you. Just looking at you makes me sick to my stomach."

Mike walked off and Lida jumped on his back trying to stop him from leaving. He flipped her over his shoulder and slammed her to the floor and knocked the air out of her. Towering over her, he stared in her eyes to say, "If you ever touch me or come near me or my family again, I will kill you. Do you hear me? I swear to God I will rip your lying throat out."

Lida was terrified. She knew he meant what he said and that broke her heart. She had finally lost the man she had been waiting years for. She stared at Mike, and he stood up and shook his head at her. He left her on the floor and walked out. His only objective now was to find Rachel. Mike headed over to Marcus' condo. He pulled up and the valet took his keys. Looking around, the lobby was empty. He hung his head low and walked to the elevator taking it to the floor they lived on.

When he got to the door, something didn't feel right. The door was halfway open and he carefully made his way in. Mike pushed the door open and saw the mess. He looked around for her and didn't see her. He began to panic as he walked around the condo searching for any clues of Rachel whereabouts. After surveying the place and coming up empty handed, Mike fell to his knees, broken and discouraged. He was overwhelmed with pain as he cried out, "Please, God, let my wife be alright."

Mike had cried so much that day that he couldn't cry anymore. When he got up, he noticed all of the blood everywhere. He wiped off everything he had touched and hurried down to the lobby trying not to be noticed. The bell hop said, "You ok, Mr.?"

Mike didn't say a word at first as he glanced up at the young man. He went a few paces and spoke, "I've lost my Rachel."

The bell hop asked, "You mean Ms. Rachel? Oh, she left earlier today. She seemed to be in a hurry."

Mike stopped dead in his tracks when he heard that. Turning around, he picked up the bell hop by his jacket and spun him around. Coming to his senses he said, "Where did she go? What did she say?"

He flooded the young man with all kinds of questions. Finally he said, "She didn't speak, but she mumbled something about getting away from here."

"Which direction did she go in?"

"Sorry, I didn't see that."

"That's ok, thank you. I'm sorry about that."

Mike got in his car and went back home. He was glad the girls were at their grandmother's house. He didn't think he could deal with them and hide what he was going through. He showered and went to bed with Rachel on his mind. Later, he got a phone call from a one eight hundred number. He was reluctant, but answered it anyway. The caller said, "Is this Mr. Michael Henderson?"

"Yes it is, who wants to know?"

"Sorry to bother you Mr. Henderson, but you signed up for Identity Protection last year and I am calling to see if you made any major transactions recently?"

"What type of transaction are we talking about?"

"Recently, a flight to Brazil was booked, and

then a hotel and other items were all purchased. Did you authorize these transactions?"

Mike paused and thought about it, then smiled, he knew it was Rachel. He replied, "Yes I did. My wife is there and the reception there is crappy. Could you please send me the information to the hotel to my email, please?"

The operator was quiet then spoke, "Did you get it, Mr. Henderson?"

"Yes I did. Thank you."

"You're welcome Mr. Henderson, please enjoy the rest of your evening."

Mike hung up and breathed a sigh of relief. At least he knew she was safe. He now had the chance to put his family back together. Everything had worked out. Marcus and Lida were both out of the picture and only time would tell if things would ever be the same again. Mike left the girls with their grandmother while he booked the next flight to Brazil to reunite with Rachel. Lida was left alone as her plan backfired. Cali made sure that Marcus was never seen or heard from again.

www.ingramcontent.com/pod-product-compliance
Lightning Source LLC
Chambersburg PA
CBHW061139170626
46809CB00003B/919